A WILL,
A WISH…
A PROPOSAL

A WILL, A WISH... A PROPOSAL

BY

JESSICA GILMORE

First published in Great Britain 2015
by Mills & Boon, an imprint of Harlequin (UK) Limited,
Large Print edition 2015
Eton House, 18-24 Paradise Road,
Richmond, Surrey, TW9 1SR

ISBN: 978-0-263-25713-7

Harlequin (UK) Limited's policy is to use papers that are natural, renewable and recyclable products and made from wood grown in sustainable forests. The logging and manufacturing processes conform to the legal environmental regulations of the country of origin.

Printed and bound in Great Britain
by CPI Antony Rowe, Chippenham, Wiltshire

To Jo, Rose and Sam—
the best godmothers any girl could ask for!
Thank you for all the love and support
you give my girl. She is very, very lucky
to have you (as am I!).
Love you all very much,
Jessica x

CHAPTER ONE

'WHAT ON EARTH were you thinking?' Max Loveday burst into the office and shook the printed out press release in his father's direction. True to form his father's chair was turned away from the desk, allowing the occupant to face the window. Apparently the view over the city 'inspired' him.

'What on earth is DL Media going to do with a dating app?'

More pertinently, where exactly were the millions of dollars his father had apparently paid out for the app going to come from? In the last year every budget had been squeezed and slashed to accommodate his father's spending spree; there was no more give in the entire company.

Steven Loveday swivelled the black leather chair around and looked at his son, his expression as guileless as that of a three-month-old baby.

It was, Max reflected, the expression he always wore when he was up to something.

And he usually was.

'Max? What a lovely surprise.'

Steven's voice was as rich as molasses and just as smooth. The kind of voice that oozed authority and paternal benevolence, as did the warm brown eyes and wide smile. It was a shame he didn't have the business acumen to match the veneer.

'When did you get back from Sydney?'

As if Max hadn't dropped him an email the second he had landed. He tightened his grip on the press release.

'Two hours ago.'

'I'm touched that you rushed over to see me but there was no need, dear boy. Take the rest of the day off.'

His father beamed at him as if he was giving Max a great treat.

'Why don't you go and visit your mother? Have you heard from her at all?'

'I can't take the day off.' Max refused to be diverted. He held up the piece of paper his PA had pressed into his hand the second he had walked into DL Media's headquarters. 'What on earth is this? Why didn't you consult me?'

His father leaned back and stared at him, his chin propped on his steepled hands. It was a look he had probably seen in a film: the wise patriarch.

'Max.' There was steel in his voice. 'I know your grandfather gave you a lot of leeway, but can I remind you this is *my* company now?'

Just.

Max held a third outright, his father another third. But, crucially, the final third, the controlling share, was held in trust by his father until he retired. Then it would go to Max. If there was a company left by then. Or if Max didn't ask the board for a vote of no confidence first…

'Grandfather did *not* give me a lot of leeway.' He could feel the paper crumple, his grip tightening even more as he fought to control his temper. It was so typical of his father to reduce all his years of hard work and training to some sort of glorified work experience. 'He trusted me and trusted my judgement.'

As he never trusted you... The words were unsaid but hung in the air.

'Look, Dad, we have a five-year plan.' A plan his father seemed determine to ignore. 'A plan that kept us profitable through the financial crisis. We need to focus on the core business strengths, not get distracted by...by...' Max sought the right diplomatic words. *Shiny new toys* might be accurate, but they were unlikely to help the situation. 'By intriguing investments.'

Steven Loveday sighed, the deep breath resonating with regret. 'The problem with your grandfather was that he had no real vision. Oh, he was a media man through and through, and he knew publishing. But books are dead, Max. It's time for us to expand, to embrace the digital world.'

Max knew his mouth was hanging open, that he was gaping at his father with an incredulous look on his face, but his poker face was eluding him. His grandfather had had no vision? Was that truly what his father thought?

'He took DL global,' he managed after a long pause. 'Made us a household name.'

A name his father seemed determined to squander. What was it they said? One generation to found, another to expand and the third to squander? It looked as if Steven Loveday was going to prove the old adage right in record time.

Max's hands curled into fists. *Not if I have anything to do with it.*

'Everyone wanted this, Max. Have you seen the concept? It's brilliant! Bored and want to go out? Just log on and see who's free—make contact, get a reservation at a mutually convenient restaurant, book your taxi home. And if the evening goes well you can even sort out a hotel room. It's going to revolutionise online dating.'

Possibly. But what did online dating have to do with publishing?

Max began to walk up and down the thickly carpeted office floor, unable to stay standing meekly in front of his father's desk like a schoolboy any longer.

'But we can't afford it. And, more crucially, it's not core business, Dad. It doesn't fit with the plan.'

'That was your grandfather's plan, not mine. We have to move with the times, Max.'

Max bit back a sigh. 'I know. Which is why we were the first to bring eBooks to the mainstream. Our interactive travel guides and language books are market leaders, and thanks to our subscription service our newspapers are actually in profit.'

He shouldn't need to be explaining this to his father. Max had always known that his father would inherit the controlling share of the company, even though Steven Loveday had only played at working over the last thirty years. He also knew how hard his grandfather had struggled with that decision, how close he had come to bypassing his son altogether for his grandson. But in the end even his hard-nosed grandfather hadn't been able to bring himself to humiliate his only child with a very public disinheriting.

And now the family business was paying the price.

The increasingly awkward silence was just beginning to stretch to excruciating when a loud and fast hip-hop tune blared out of the phone on his father's desk. It was the kind of ringtone Max would expect from a streetwise fifteen-year-old, not a fifty-eight-year-old man in a hand-made suit and silk tie, but his father's eyes lit up as he grabbed the telephone, his body swaying a little to the furious beat.

'Sweetie?'

Max could just make out a giggle from the caller. Not that he needed to hear the voice to know who it was. The inappropriate ringtone, the soppy expression on his father's face, the nauseating tone of his voice…

It had been six months. If his father was playing true to form he should be getting bored with his latest crush by now. But then none of this latest infatuation was running true to form. Not bringing it out in the open, not leaving Max's mother and setting up a love-nest in a Hartford penthouse… No, Steven Loveday's little affairs of the heart were usually as brief as they were intense, but they were always, *always* clandestine.

This…? This almost felt…well, *serious.*

His father looked over at Max. 'Mandy sends her love.'

Max muttered something inaudible even to himself. What was the etiquette here? Just what *did* you say to your father's mistress? Especially a mistress several years younger than yourself—and your own ex-PA. She'd giggled a lot less then.

To occupy himself while his father continued to croon sweet nothings down the phone, he pulled out his own phone and began to scroll through the long list of emails. As usual they were multiplying like the Hydra's head: ten springing forth for each one he deleted. His father's name might top the letterhead, but Max's workload seemed to have tripled in the last year no matter how many sixteen-hour days and seven-day weeks he pulled.

Delete, forward, mark for attention, delete, *definitely* delete... He paused. Another missive from Ellie Scott. What did Miss Prim and Proper want now?

Max had developed a picture of Ellie Scott over the last two months of mostly one-sided emails. She had to be of a similar age to his recently deceased great-aunt, probably wore tweed and had those horned reading glasses. In tortoiseshell.

He bet that she played bridge, golfed in sturdy brogues and breakfasted on kippers and anaemic toast.

Okay, he had based her on all those old classic series featuring British spinsters of a certain age. But the bossy, imperative, clipped tone of her emails made him pretty certain he couldn't be that far off in his estimate.

And she lived to plague him. Her requests for information, agreement, input and, worst of all, his actual presence had upped from one a week to almost daily. Sure, the money his great-aunt had left to start a literary festival in a tiny village in the middle of nowhere might seem important to Miss Scott, but he had actual *real* work to do. At some point he was going to have to see if he could delegate or refuse the trustee post he had been bequeathed. *And* get somebody to sort out the house that was part of the same unwanted legacy.

There was just no time for anything that didn't involve clearing up after his father.

Max's finger didn't even pause as he pressed 'delete'. He moved on, reading another and another, and—hang on a minute. His eyes flicked back up the screen as he reread one, barely able to believe the words dancing in front of his eyes.

Irregularity...
Share of the company...
Your great-aunt...
Twenty-five per cent.

Max blinked, casting a quick glance over at his father. Did he know? Could it possibly be true that his recently deceased great-aunt had kept hold of her twenty-five per cent of DL Media even after she had walked away from her work and her family? The same great-aunt who had left her house and belongings to *him*? This could change everything.

Maybe Miss Scott's luck was in. A trip to Cornwall might be exactly what the lawyer ordered.

'Sorry about that.' His father's expression was a discomfiting mixture of slightly sheepish and sappy. 'Max, I would really appreciate it if you had a word with your mother.'

Here they went again. How many times had Max been asked to broker a rapprochement in the constant battlefield that was his parents' marriage? Every time he swore never to do it again. But someone had to be the responsible one in the family, and somehow, even when he could still measure his age in single digits, that person had had to be him.

But not this time.

'I'm sure she would rather hear from you.'

The sappy look on his dad's face faded. He was completely sheepish now, avoiding Max's eye and fiddling with the paperclips on his desk. 'My attorney has told me not to speak to her directly.'

Time stopped for one long second, the office freezing like a paused scene in a movie.

'Attorney? Dad, what on earth do you need an attorney for?'

'You're going to be a big brother.'

Max stopped in the middle of a breath. He was *what*?

'Mandy's pregnant and we're engaged. The second your mother stops being unreasonable about terms and we can get a divorce I'll be getting married. I'd like you to be my best man.'

His father beamed, as if he were conferring a huge honour on Max.

'Divorce?' Max shook his head as if he could magically *un*-hear the words, pushing the whole 'big brother' situation far away into a place where he didn't have to think about it or deal with it. 'Come on, Dad. How many times have you fallen in love, only to realise it's Mum you need?'

Max could think of at least eight occasions without trying—but his dad had never mentioned attorneys before.

'Max, she's demanding fifty per cent of my share of the company. And she wants it in cash if possible. DL can't afford that kind of settlement and *I* sure as hell can't. You have to talk her down. She'll listen to you.'

She wanted *what*? This was exactly what DL Media didn't need. An expensive and very public divorce. Max had two choices: help his dad, or involve the board and wrestle control of that crucial third of the company from his dad.

Either option meant public scrutiny, gossip, tearing the family apart. Everything his grandfather had trusted Max to prevent.

A pulse was throbbing in his temple, the blood thrumming in his veins. Talk to his mother, to the board, to his dad, go over the books yet again and try and work out how to put the company back on an even keel. There were no easy answers. Hell, right now he'd settle for *difficult* answers.

Steven Loveday was still looking at him, appeal in his eyes, but Max couldn't, *wouldn't* meet his gaze. Instead he found himself fixated on the large watercolour on the opposite wall: the only one of his grandfather's possessions to survive the recent office refurbishment. Blue skies smiled down on white-crested seas as green cliffs soared high above the curve of the harbour. Trengarth. The village his great-grandfather had left behind all those years ago. Max could almost smell the salt in the air, hear the waves crashing on the shore.

'I'm away for the next two weeks. The London office is shouting out for some guidance, and I need to sort out Great-Aunt Demelza's inheritance. You're on your own with this one, Dad. And for goodness' sake, don't throw everything away for an infatuation.'

He swivelled on his heel and walked towards the door, not flinching as his father called desperately after him. 'It's different this time, Max. I love her. I really do.'

How many times had he heard that one? His father's need to live up to their surname had caused more than enough problems in the Loveday family.

Love? No, thank you. Max had stopped believing in that long before his voice had broken, along with Father Christmas and life being fair. It was time his father grew up and accepted that family, position and the business came first. It was a lesson Max had learned years ago.

'Ellie, dear, I've been thinking about the literary festival.'

Ellie Scott turned around from the shelf she was rearranging, managing—*just*—not to roll her eyes.

It wasn't that she wanted to stifle independent thought in Trengarth. She didn't even want to stifle it in her shop—after all, part of the joy of running a bookshop was seeing people's worlds opening out, watching their horizons expanding. But every time her assistant—her hard-working, good-hearted and extremely able assistant, she reminded herself for the three billionth time—uttered those words she wanted to jump in a boat and sail as far out to sea as possible. Or possibly send Mrs Trelawney out in it, all the way across the ocean.

'That's great, Mrs Trelawney. Make sure you hold on to those thoughts. I'll need to start planning it very soon.'

Her assistant put down her duster and sniffed. 'So you say, Ellie…so you say. Oh, I've been defending you. "Yes, she's an incomer," I've said. "Yes, it's odd that old Miss Loveday left her money to Ellie and not to somebody born and bred here. But," I said, "she has the interests of Trengarth at heart."'

Ellie couldn't hold in her sigh any longer. 'Mrs Trelawney, you know as well as I do that I *can't* do anything. There are two trustees and we have to act together. My hands are tied until Miss Loveday's nephew deigns to honour us with his presence. And, *yes*,' she added as Mrs Trelawney's mouth opened. 'I have emailed, written and begged the solicitors to contact him. I am as keen to get started as you are.'

'Keen to give up a small fortune?' The older woman lifted her eyes up to the heavens, eloquently expressing just how implausible she thought that was.

Was there any point in explaining yet again that Miss Loveday hadn't actually left her fortune to Ellie personally, and that Ellie wasn't sitting on a big pile of cash, cackling from her high tower at the poverty stricken villagers below? The bequest's wording was very clear: the money had been left in trust to Ellie and the absent second trustee for the purposes of establishing an annual literary festival in the Cornish village.

Of course not every inhabitant of the small fishing village felt that a festival was the best thing to benefit the community, and most of them seemed to hold Ellie solely responsible for Demelza Loveday's edict. In vain had Ellie argued that she was powerless to spend the money elsewhere, sympathetic as she was to the competing claims of needing a new playground and refurbishing the village hall—but her hands were tied.

'Look, Mrs Trelawney. I know how keen you are to get started, and how many excellent ideas you have. I promise you that if Miss Loveday's nephew does not contact me in the next month then I will go to America myself and force him to co-operate.'

'Hmm.' The sound spoke volumes, as did the accompanying and very thorough dusting of already spotless shelves.

Ellie didn't blame Mrs Trelawney for being unconvinced. Truthfully, she had no idea how to get the elusive Max Loveday *to* co-operate. Tempting as it was to imagine herself striding into his New York penthouse and marching him over to an aeroplane, she knew full well that sending yet another strongly worded email was about as forceful as she was likely to get.

Not to mention that she didn't actually know where he lived. But if she was going to daydream she might as well make it as glamorous as possible.

Ellie stepped back and stared critically at the

display shelf, temptingly filled with the perfect books to read on the wide, sandy Trengarth beach—or to curl up with if the weather was uncooperative. Just one week until the schools broke up and the season started in full. It was such a short season. Trengarth certainly needed something to keep the village on the tourism radar throughout the rest of the year. Maybe this festival was part of the answer.

If they could just get started.

Ellie stole a glance over at her assistant. Her heart was in the right place. Mrs Trelawney had lived in the village all her life. It must be heartbreaking for her to see it so empty in the winter months, with so many houses now second homes and closed from October through to Easter.

'If I can't get an answer in the next two weeks then I will look into getting him replaced. There must be *something* the solicitors can do if he simply won't take on his responsibilities. But the last thing I want to do is spend some of the bequest on legal fees. It's only been a few months. I think we just need to be a little patient a little longer.'

Besides, the elusive Max Loveday worked for

DL Media, one of the big six publishing giants. Ellie had no idea if he was an editor, an accountant or the mail boy, but whatever he did he was bound to have some contacts. More than the sole proprietor of a small independent bookshop at the end of the earth.

The bell over the door jangled and Ellie turned around, grateful for the opportunity to break off the awkward conversation.

Not that the newcomer looked as if he was going to make her day any easier, judging by the firm line of his mouth and the expression of distaste as he looked around the book-lined room from his vantage position by the door.

It was a shame, because under the scowl he was really rather nice to look at. Ellie's usual clientele were families and the older villagers. It wasn't often that handsome, youngish men came her way, and he was both. Definitely under thirty, she decided, and tall, with close-cut dark hair, a roughly stubbled chin and eyes so lightly brown they were almost caramel.

But the expression in the eyes was hard and it was focussed right onto Mrs Trelawney.

What on earth had her assistant been up to now? Ellie knew there was some kind of leadership battle on the Village in Bloom committee, but she wouldn't have expected the man at the door to be involved.

Although several young and trendy gardeners *had* recently set up in the vicinity. Maybe he was very passionate about native species and tasteful colour combinations?

'Miss Scott?'

Unease curdled Ellie's stomach at the curt tone, and she had to force herself not to take a step back. *This is your shop*, she told herself, folding her hands into tight fists. *Nobody can tell you what to do. Not any more.*

'I'm Ellie Scott.' She had to release her assistant from that gimlet glare. Not that Mrs Trelawney looked in need of help. Her own gaze was just as hard and cold. 'Can I help?'

'You?'

The faint tone of incredulity didn't endear him any further to Ellie, and nor did the quick glance that raked her up and down in one fast, judgemental dismissal.

'You can't be. You're just a girl.'

'Thank you, but at twenty-five I'm quite grown up.'

His voice was unmistakably American which meant, surely, that here at last was the other trustee. Tired and jetlagged, probably, which explained the attitude. Coffee and a slice of cake would soon set him to rights.

Ellie held out her hand. 'Please, call me Ellie. You must be Max. It's lovely to meet you.'

'*You're* the woman my great-aunt left half her fortune to?'

His face had whitened, all except his eyes, which were a dark, scorching gold.

'Tell me, Miss Scott…' He made no move to take her hand, just stood looking at her as if she had turned into a toad, ice frosting every syllable. 'Which do you think is worse? Seducing an older married man for his money or befriending an elderly lady for hers?'

He folded his arms and stared at her.

'Any thoughts?'

CHAPTER TWO

MAX HADN'T INTENDED to go in all guns blazing. In fact he had entered the bookshop with just two intentions: to pick up the keys to the house his great-aunt had left him and to make it very clear to the domineering Miss Scott that the next step in sorting out his great-aunt's quixotic will would be at *his* instigation and in *his* time frame.

Only he had been wrong-footed at the start. Where was the hearty spinster of his imagination? He certainly hadn't been expecting this thin, neatly dressed pale girl. She was almost mousy, although there *was* a delicate beauty in her huge brown eyes, in the neatly brushed sweep of her light brown hair that looked dull at first glance but, he noticed as the sunlight fell on it, was actually a mass of toffee and dark gold.

She didn't look like a con artist. She looked like the little match girl. Maybe that was the point.

Maybe inspiring pity was her weapon. He had thought, assumed, that his co-trustee was an old friend of Great-Aunt Demelza. Not a girl younger than Max himself. Her youth was all too painfully reminiscent of his father's recent insanity, even if Ellie Scott seemed to be missing some of Mandy's more obvious attributes.

The silence stretched long, thin, almost unbearable before Ellie broke it. 'I beg your pardon?'

There was a shakiness in her voice but she stayed her ground, the large eyes fixed on him with painful intensity.

Max was shocked by a rush of guilt. It was like shooting Bambi.

'I think you heard.'

He was uneasily aware that they had an audience. The angular, tweed-clad old lady he had assumed was Ellie Scott was standing guard by the counter, a duster held threateningly in one hand, her sharp eyes darting expectantly from one to the other like a tennis umpire. He should give her some popcorn and a large soda to help her fully enjoy the show.

'I was giving you a chance to backtrack or apologise.'

Ellie Scott's voice had grown stronger, and for the first time he had a chance to notice her pointed chin and firm, straight eyebrows, both suggesting a subtle strength of character.

'But if you have no intention of doing either than I suggest you leave and come back when you find your manners.'

It was his turn to think he'd misheard. 'What?'

'You heard me. Leave. And unless you're willing to be polite don't come back.'

Max glared at her, but although there was a slight tremor in her lightly clenched hands Ellie Scott didn't move. Fine.

He walked back over to the door and wrenched it open. 'This isn't over, honey,' he warned her. 'I will find out exactly how you manoeuvred your way into my great-aunt's good graces and I will get back every penny you conned out of her.'

The jaunty bell jangled as he closed the door behind him. Firmly.

The calendar said it was July, but the Cornish weather had obviously decided to play unseasonal and Max, who had left a humid heatwave behind in Connecticut, was hit by a cold gust of wind, shooting straight through the thin cotton of his T-shirt, goose-pimpling his arms and shocking him straight to his bones.

And sweeping the anger clear out of his head.

What on earth had he been thinking? Or, as it turned out, *not* thinking. *Damn.* Somehow he had completely misfired.

Max took a deep breath, the salty tang of sea air filling his lungs. He shouldn't have gone straight into the shop after the long flight and even longer drive from Gatwick airport to this sleepy Cornish corner. Not with the adrenaline still pumping through his veins. Not with the scene with his father still playing through his head.

Who knew what folly his father would commit without Max keeping an eye on him? Where his mother's anger and sense of betrayal would drag them down to?

But that was their problem. DL Media was his sole concern now.

Max began to wander down the steep, narrow sidewalk. It felt as if he had reached the ends of the earth during the last three hours of his drive through the most western and southern parts of England. A drive that had brought him right here, to the place his great-grandfather had left behind, shaking off his family ties, the blood and memories of the Great War and England, when he had crossed the channel to start a whole new life.

And now Max had ended up back here. Funny how circular life could be...

Pivoting slowly, Max took a moment to see just where *'here'* was. The briny smell might take him back to holidays spent on the Cape, but Trengarth was as different from the flat dunes of Cape Cod as American football was from soccer.

The small bookshop was one of several higgledy-piggledy terraces on a steep narrow road winding up the cliff. At the top of the cliff, imperiously looking down onto the bay and dominating the smaller houses dotted around it, was a white circular house: his Great-Aunt Demelza's house. The house she had left to him. A house where hopefully there would be coffee, some food. A bed. A solution.

If he carried on heading down he would reach

the seafront and the narrow road running alongside the ocean. Turn left and the old harbour curved out to sea, still filled with fishing boats. All the cruisers and yachts were moored further out. Above the harbour the old fishermen's cottages were built up the cliff: a riotous mixture of colours and styles.

Turn right and several more shops faced on to the road before it stopped abruptly at the causeway leading to the wide beach where, despite or because of the weather, surfers were bobbing up and down in the waves, looking like small, sleek seals.

Give him an hour and he could join them. He could take a board out…hire a boat. Forget his cares in the cold tang of the ocean.

Max smiled wryly. If only he could. Pretend he was just another American tourist retracing his roots, shrugging off the responsibilities he carried. But, like Atlas, he was never going to be relieved of his heavy burden.

It *was* a pretty place. And weirdly familiar—although maybe not that weird. After all, his grandfather had had several watercolours of almost exactly this view hanging in his study. Yes, there were definitely worse places to work out a way forward.

Only to do that he needed to get into that large white house. And according to the solicitor he had emailed from the plane, Ellie Scott was holding the keys to that very house. Which meant he was going to have to eat some humble pie. Max was normally quite a fan of pie, but that was not a flavour he enjoyed.

'Suck it up, Max,' he muttered to a low-flying seagull, which was eyeing him hopefully. 'Suck it up.'

He was going to have to go back to the bookshop and start the whole acquaintance again.

Ellie was doing her best to damp down the dismaying swirl in her stomach and get on with her day.

She hadn't caved, had she? Hadn't trembled or wept or tried to pacify him? She had stayed calm and collected and in control. On the outside, at least. Only she knew that right now she wanted nothing more than to sink into the old rocking chair in the corner of the childcare section and indulge in a pathetic bout of tears.

The sneering tone, the cold, scornful expression had triggered far more feelings than she cared to admit. She had spent three years trying to pacify that exact tone, that exact look—and the next three years trying to forget. In just five minutes Max Loveday had brought it all vividly back.

Darn him—and darn her shaky knees and trembling hands, giving away her inner turmoil. She'd thought she was further on than this. Stronger than this.

Ellie had never thought she would be quite so glad for Mrs Trelawney's presence, but right now the woman was her safety net. While she sat there, busily typing away on her phone, no doubt ensuring that every single person in Trengarth was fully updated on the morning's events, Ellie had no option but to hold things together.

Instead she switched on the coffee machine and unpacked the cakes she had picked up earlier from the Boat House café on the harbour.

Ellie had always dreamed of a huge bookshop,

packed with hidden corners, secret nooks, and supplemented by a welcoming café full of tasty treats. What she had was a shop which, like all the shops in Trengarth, was daintily proportioned. Fitting in all the books she wanted to stock in the snug space was enough of a challenge. A café would be a definite step too far. She had compromised with a long counter by the till heaped with a tempting array of locally made scones and cakes and a state-of-the-art coffee machine. Buying in the cakes meant she didn't have to sacrifice precious stock space for a kitchen.

It took just a few moments to arrange the flapjacks, Cornish fairing biscuits, brightly coloured cupcakes and scones onto vintage cake stands and cover them with the glass domes she used to keep them fresh.

'We have walnut, orange and cheese scones.' She deliberately spoke aloud as she began to chalk up the varieties onto the blackboard she kept propped on the table, hoping Mrs Trelawney would take the hint, stop texting and start working. 'The cupcakes are vanilla and the big cake is...let me see...yep, carrot and orange.'

'It's a bit early for cake…'

The drawling accent made her stop and stiffen.

'But I'll take a walnut scone and a coffee. Please.'

The last word was *so* evidently an afterthought.

Ellie smiled sweetly as she swivelled round. No way was she going to give him the satisfaction of seeing how uncomfortable he'd made her.

'It's self-service and pay at the till. You, however, are barred. You'll have to get your coffee somewhere else.'

'Look…' Max Loveday looked meaningfully over at Mrs Trelawney. 'Can we talk? In private?'

Ellie's heart began to pick up speed, her pulse hammering. No way was she going anywhere alone with this man. He might be smiling now, but she wasn't fooled.

'I don't think so. You had no problem insulting me in front of my assistant. I'm sure she can't wait to hear round two.'

He closed his eyes briefly. 'Fair point.'

'Oh, good.' She hadn't expected him to capitulate so easily. It was an unexpected and unwanted point in his favour. 'Go on, then. Say whatever it is you have to say.'

'I was out of line.'

Ellie folded her arms and raised her eyebrows. If Max Loveday thought he was getting away with anything short of a full-on grovel he could think again.

'Yes...?' she prompted.

'And I'm sorry. It's no excuse, but my family is going through some stuff right now and I'm a little het-up about it.'

'Tell me, Mr Loveday...' Ellie deliberately parroted his words back to him. 'Which is worse? Seducing a family man for his money or conning an old lady out of her cash? And which are you accusing *me* of?'

As if she didn't know. Well, if she'd conned the old lady he'd been right there with her; he was joint trustee after all.

'I think they're both pretty vile.' There was a bleakness in his voice, and when his eyes rested on Ellie the hardness in them unnerved her. He hadn't come back because he was stricken with remorse. He still thought her guilty.

'So do I.' The look of surprise on his face gave her courage. 'I also think making slanderous accusations against strangers and proffering fake apologies in order to get the keys to a house and a cup of coffee is pretty out of order. What do you say to *that*, Mr Loveday?'

'I'm prepared to pay for the coffee.'

It wasn't much of a retort but it was the best he could do when he was firmly in the wrong—as far as manners were concerned—and so tired that the wooden floor was beginning to look more than a little inviting. Flying Sydney to Boston to Hartford and then on to England in just a few days had left him in a grey smog that even first-class sleep pods hadn't quite been able to dispel.

'Look, you have to admit my great-aunt's will is pretty unusual. Leaving her entire fortune in the hands of a virtual stranger.'

The large brown eyes darkened with something that looked very much like scorn. It wasn't an expression Max was used to seeing in anybody's eyes and it stung more than he expected.

'Yes, she said more than once that she wished

she knew her great-nephew more. I thought this was her way of trying to include you.'

Damn her, he hadn't meant *himself*—and he would bet a much needed good night's sleep she knew that full well.

'It was her money to leave as she liked. I didn't expect to inherit a penny. Nor do I need to. If she wanted to leave it all to charity that's one thing. But this...? This is craziness. Leaving it to you... to found a festival. I didn't ask to be involved.'

He just couldn't comprehend it. What on earth had his great-aunt been thinking? What did he know or care about a little village on the edge of the ocean?

'She didn't actually leave the money to me, to you or to *us*.'

Ellie sounded completely exasperated. Max got the feeling it wasn't the first time she'd had this conversation.

'I can't touch a penny without your say-so and vice versa—and we're both completely accountable to the executors. There is no fraud here, Mr Loveday, and no coercion. Nothing at all except a slightly odd request made by a whimsical elderly lady. Didn't you read the will?'

'I read enough to know that she left you this shop.'

No coercion, indeed. Ellie Scott wasn't just a trustee she was a beneficiary: inheriting the shop and the flat above it. The flat she already currently resided in, according to the will. It was all very neat.

'Yes…' The brightness dimmed from her eyes, and it was as if the sun had gone behind a cloud. 'She was always good to me. She was my godmother. Did you know that? My grandmother's best friend, and my own good, dear friend. I will always be grateful to her. For everything.'

'Your godmother?'

Damn, he had come into the whole situation blind and it was completely unlike him. It was sloppy, led to mistakes.

'Yes. But even more importantly she was your great-aunt. Which is why she wanted you involved in her legacy, why she left you the house. It was the house her father was born in, apparently. And *his* father was some kind of big deal sea captain. He would have been...what? Your great-great-grandfather?'

'Yes, although I don't know anything about him or about anything to do with the English side of the family. A sea captain?' A reluctant smile curved his lips. He had been in Cornwall all of an hour and had already discovered some unknown family history. 'My grandfather took me sailing all the time. He had a house on the Cape. Said he always slept best when he could hear the sea. Must be in our blood.'

'You can hear the sea from every room in The Round House too. Maybe my godmother knew what she was doing when she left the house to you.'

'Maybe.'

It was a nice idea. But, *really*? A house? In Cornwall? A seven-hour flight and a tedious long drive from his home. It would have been far simpler if Great-Aunt Demelza had instructed her solicitors to liquefy the whole estate and endowed a wing at her favourite museum or hospital. *That* was how philanthropy worked. Not this messy, getting involved business.

Although it *was* kind of cool to find out about his distant Cornish heritage. A sea captain… Maybe there was a photo back at the house.

A voice broke in from the corner and Max jumped. He'd forgotten about their audience.

'This is all very entertaining. But what I want to know, Ellie, is are you planning to actually start this festival or not?'

Ellie looked at him, her face composed. 'I don't think that's up to me any more, Mrs Trelawney. Well, Mr Loveday? Are you willing to work with me? Or do we need to call the solicitors in and find a way around the trust?'

'I can't just drop everything, Miss Scott. I have a very busy job. A job in Connecticut. Across the ocean. I can't walk away to spend weeks playing benefactor by the sea.'

But even as he spoke the words a chill shivered through him. What did the next few months hold? Could he find a way to make his father toe the line—or was he going to have to force a vote at the board?

He would win. He knew many of the board members shared his misgivings. But then what?

His already fragile relationship with his father would be irrevocably shattered.

It was a price he was willing to pay. And if his great-aunt's house *did* hold the key to an easy win then the least he could do was help get her dream started while he was here. His mouth twisted. It wasn't as easy to walk away from family obligations as he'd thought, even when the family member was a stranger *and* deceased.

'I can give you two weeks. Although I'll be in London some of that time. Take it or leave it.'

Ellie's cool gaze was fixed on him. As if she could see straight into the heart of him—and see all that was missing.

'Fine.'

'So I can set up a meeting?' asked Mrs Trelawney. 'I have a lot of ideas and I know many other people do too.' Ellie's assistant had given up any pretence of working, her eyes bright as she leaned onto the counter. 'We could have a theme. Or base it on a genre? A murder mystery with actors? Or should we have it food-related. There could be baking competitions—make your favourite literary cake.'

Your favourite *what*? Max tried to avoid catching Ellie's eye but it was impossible to look away. The serious, slightly sad expression had disappeared, to be replaced by a mischievous smile lurking in the deep brown depths of her large eyes.

He could feel an answering gleam in his own eyes, and his mouth wanted to smile in response, to try and coax a grin out of her, but he kept his face as calm and sincere as he could, trying to keep all his focus on Mrs Trelawney.

But he couldn't stop his gaze sliding across to watch Ellie's reaction. She was leaning against a bookcase, her arms folded as her face sparkled in amusement.

'They are excellent ideas,' he managed, and was rewarded by the quick upturn of her full mouth and the intriguing hint of a dimple in one pale cheek. 'But we are at a very early stage. I think we need to talk to the solicitors and look at funds before we…ah…appoint a committee. I do hope you can manage to hold on to those ideas for just a little longer?'

'Well, yes.' Mrs Trelawney's cheeks were pink. 'Of course. I can make a list. I have a lot of ideas.'

'I for one can believe it.' Ellie pushed away from the shelves in one graceful movement. 'I'm expecting a delivery in an hour, Mrs Trelawney, so now would be a good time for you to take your break if that's convenient?'

'My break?' Mrs Trelawney's eyes moved from Max to Ellie and back again before she reluctantly nodded.

Ellie didn't speak again until her assistant had collected her bag and left the shop. 'Poor Mrs T. She's torn between being the first to spread the gossip and fear of missing out on any more. Still, the arrival of Demelza Loveday's mysterious American great-nephew should give her enough to be getting on with. And...' there was a tart note in her voice '...you certainly managed to stir things up when you walked into my shop.'

This was his chance to apologise. Max still wasn't entirely sure what to make of Ellie Scott, but what had his grandfather always said? It was much easier to judge from the inside rather than out in the cold. 'I had my reasons. But they didn't really have anything to do with you. I'm sorry.'

Ellie pushed back a piece of hair that had fallen out of the clip confining the long tresses. 'I can't say that's okay, because it isn't. But I'm willing to give you a second chance. It's going to be hard enough for two incomers to win the support of a place like Trengarth as it is, without being at war ourselves.'

'You're an incomer?' Max wasn't exactly an expert on British accents and Ellie sounded just as he'd expected her to: like the heroine of one of those awful films where girls wore bonnets and the men tights, all speaking with clipped vowels and clear enunciation.

'I spent most of my childhood summers here, and I've lived here for the last three years, but I'll still be an incomer in thirty.' She hesitated. 'Look, I'll be honest. I would be more than happy to see you off the premises and never have to deal with you again, but we have to work together for the next two weeks. You must be tired and jet-lagged. Why don't you go and rest now and come back tomorrow? We'll start again.'

Her words were conciliatory, her voice confident, but there was a wariness in her posture.

She was slightly turned away, the slim shoulders a little hunched, and her arms were protectively wrapped around her. She was afraid of something. Afraid of him? Of what he might discover? Maybe she wasn't as innocent as she appeared.

He'd been putting this off long enough, distracted by his father's extra-marital shenanigans and the all-consuming pressures of living up to the family legacy. It was time to talk to the solicitors, read the damn will properly and find out just what Ellie Scott was hiding.

'That is a very generous offer. Thank you.'

Ellie exhaled on a visible sigh of relief.

'Then I'll see you back here tomorrow. I'll telephone the solicitors and see if they can fit us in. Do you know how to get to the house?'

She walked around the counter, crouching down and disappearing from view before handing him a set of keys.

They were old-fashioned iron keys. Heavy and unwieldy. 'I'll find my way, thanks. See you later, honey.'

It was both a promise and a threat—and he was pretty sure she knew it.

CHAPTER THREE

THE SHOP HAD been busy. So busy Ellie hadn't had a moment to dwell on the morning's encounter. And even though she knew a fair few of her customers had come in to try and prise information about Max Loveday out of her—or out of the far more forthcoming Mrs Trelawney—they had all bought something, even if it was just a coffee.

Slowly Ellie began to tidy up, knowing that she was deliberately putting off the moment when she would head upstairs. She loved her flat, and normally she loved the silence, the space, the solitude. Knowing it was hers to do with as she pleased. But this evening she dreaded the time alone. She knew she would relive every cutting remark, every look, every moment of her bruising encounter with Max Loveday. And that inevitably her thoughts would turn to her ex-fiancé. It wasn't a place she wanted to go.

And tomorrow she would have to deal with Max all over again.

As always, the ritual of shutting up shop soothed her. From the day she had opened it the shop had been a sanctuary. *Her* sanctuary. She had planned and designed every feature, every reading nook and display, had painted the walls, hung the pictures, shelved each and every book. Had even chosen the temperamental diva of a coffee machine, which needed twenty minutes of cleaning and wiping before she could put it to bed, and sanded the wood she used for a counter.

She had been able to indulge her love of colour, of posters, of clutter. Nobody expected a bookshop to be tastefully minimalist.

By seven o'clock Ellie could put it off no longer. Every book was in its rightful place. Even the preschool picture books were neatly lined up in alphabetical order. A futile task—it needed just one three-year-old to return the entire rack to chaos.

The shelves were gleaming and dust-free, the cushions on sofas, chairs and benches were shaken out and plumped up, the floor was swept and the leftover cakes had been boxed away. She'd even counted the cash and reconciled the till.

There was literally nothing left to do.

Except leave.

Ellie switched the lights off and stood for a moment, admiring the neatness of the room in the evening light. 'Thank you,' she whispered. If Demelza Loveday hadn't encouraged her to follow her dreams, hadn't rented her the shop, where would Ellie be now?

And, like the fairy godmother she'd been, Miss Loveday had ensured that Ellie could always stay here, always be safe. The shop and the flat were hers. Nobody could ever take them away from her. And, no matter what Max Loveday thought, it hadn't been Ellie's idea. The legacy was a wonderful, thoughtful gift—and it had been a complete surprise. The one bright moment in the grey weeks following Miss Loveday's death and the unwelcome burden of the trust.

A rap at the closed door made her jump. The shop was evidently closed. The sign said so, the shutter was drawn, the lights dimmed right down in the two bay windows. But it wouldn't be the first time someone had needed an emergency gift. That was the thing about small towns: you were never really fully closed.

'Coming,' she called as she stepped over to the door, untwisting the lock and shooting back the two bolts before cautiously opening it…just a few centimetres. Not that there had ever been any robbery beyond the odd bit of shoplifting in Trengarth's small high street.

Ellie's hands tightened on the doorframe as she took in the lean, tall figure, the close-cut dark hair and stubbled chin.

She swallowed. Hard. 'I didn't think we were meeting until tomorrow.' She didn't open the door wider or invite him to come in.

'I wanted to apologise again.' Max held up a bottle of red wine. 'I found this in Great-Aunt Demelza's wine cellar. She had quite a collection.'

'It's your collection now.' Ellie didn't reach out and take the bottle, her hands still firmly clasping the door, keeping it just ajar.

Max pulled a face. 'I can't quite get my head

around that. It seemed pretty intrusive, just walking in and showering in the guest en-suite bathroom, looking around at all her stuff. I mean, I didn't actually know her.'

Showering? Ellie immediately tried to push that particular image out of her mind but it lingered there. A fall of water, right onto a tanned, lean torso… Her fingers tightened as her stomach swooped. Her libido had been dead for years. Did it *have* to choose right this moment to resuscitate itself?

'I was planning on chocolates as well, but the shop is shut.' He gestured behind him to the small all-purpose supermarket. 'They were shut this morning as well. Do they *ever* open?'

Ellie looked over at the firmly drawn shutters, grateful for a chance to think about anything but long, steamy showers. 'They do open for longer in the school holidays, but otherwise the hours are a little limiting. It's okay if you know them, but it can be frustrating for tourists—and then Mr Whitehead complains that people drive to the next town and use the bigger supermarkets.'

There. That was a perfectly safe, inane and

even dull comment. Libido back in check. She was most definitely *not* looking at the golden tan on his arms, nor noticing the muscle definition under his T-shirt. No, not at all.

'You really didn't have to,' she hurried on, forcing her eyes back up and focussing firmly on his ear. No one could have inappropriate thoughts about an ear, could they? 'Really.'

'I think I did.' His smile was rueful. 'I managed a few hours' sleep on the couch and when I woke up I felt just terrible. Not just because of the jet-lag. My grandfather would have been horrified if he had heard me speak to a lady that way. He brought me up better than that.'

Grandfather? Not parents? Interesting...

'Anyway, I thought I'd make amends and get some air...have a look at this town my great-grandfather crossed an ocean to escape. I don't suppose you'd like to join me? Show me around?'

No, she most definitely would not. In fact she had a very important date with the new edition of *Anne of Green Gables* she had unpacked that very morning: hardback, illustrated and annotated. She also had a quarter-bottle of wine, a piece of salmon and some salad.

Another crazy evening in the Scott household of one.

Would anything change if she threw caution to the wind and went out for a walk before dinner, book, bath and bed? In fact she often took an evening walk. The only real difference would be her companion.

He was her beloved godmother's nephew. Surely Demelza would have wanted her to make him welcome, no matter how bad his first impression? Hadn't she just been remembering just how much she owed her benefactress? She really should replay the debt. Besides, he was trying to make amends. She wasn't used to that.

A flutter started low down in her stomach. For so many years she had been told she was in the wrong, no matter what the reality. A man admitting his mistake was a novel experience.

Ellie swung the door open and stood back. 'Come in,' she invited him. 'I just need to change my shoes and grab my bag.'

It would have been nice to have some more notice. She was still in the grey velvet skinny jeans she had pulled on that morning, teamed with a purple flowered tunic. Her hair was neatly tucked back in a clip and she wasn't wearing any make-up. Not that she usually did for work, but she suddenly wished she had some armour...even if it was just a coat of mascara.

Ellie waited as Max stepped through the door, moving from one foot to the other in indecision. She needed to go upstairs, but she seldom invited other people into her flat. Would it be odd to leave him kicking his heels in the shop while she grabbed a cardigan and quickly brushed out her hair? At least there was plenty for him to read.

'You might as well come up.'

Not the most gracious invitation, but he didn't need asking twice, following her through the dark bookshop to the discreet wooden door at the back of the shop which marked the line between home and work.

Ellie was used to the narrow, low staircase, but she could sense Max taking it more slowly, his head brushing the ceiling as the staircase turned. He breathed an audible sigh of relief when he arrived at the top of the staircase with the top of his head still intact.

The narrow staircase curved and continued up to the third storey, where her bedroom, study and bathroom were situated, but she stepped out into the flat's main hallway. It was simply decorated in a light olive-green, with the colour picked up in the striped runner covering polished floor-boards. At the far end a window overlooked the street. Next to it a row of pegs was covered with an assortment of her jackets, coats and scarves; boots and shoes were lined up beneath them.

On her right the kitchen door was slightly ajar. Her unwashed breakfast dishes were still piled on the side. Ellie fought the urge to shut the door, to hide them. In the years she had lived with her ex, Simon, she had learned quickly to tidy up all detritus straight away. Leaving dirty dishes out for a few hours was a small act of rebellion, but it made the flat hers, the kitchen hers. A sign that she was free of his control.

'Just go straight ahead.' She tried to keep her voice light, to hide what a big deal this was.

The living room ran the full length of the

building, with a window at either end flooding the long room with evening light. A red velvet three-seater couch and matching loveseat were arranged at right angles at one end of the room; a small dining table with four chairs stood at the other. The walls were plain white, but she had injected colour with dozens of framed posters: her favourites from her last three years of book-selling.

Max stepped inside and looked around. ‘No books?’ He sounded surprised.

Ellie laughed, a little nervously. ‘Oh, plenty of books. I keep them on the landing and in the study. I thought being surrounded by books all day and all night would probably turn me into a *real* hermit instead of practically being one.’

‘Here.’ He proffered the wine to her. ‘Please, take it.’

Ellie looked at it. She needed to make her position clear before she accepted the wine…before she showed him round the village. Before she was distracted again by the evening sun on a bare arm or visions of showers. She had promised herself that she would always speak out, always be honest, never allow herself to be pushed back into being the quiet, submissive ghost she had been with Simon.

Only it wasn't quite so easy in practice.

She took a deep breath, her fingers linking, twisting as she did so. 'I'll be honest, Mr Loveday…'

His eyebrows flew up at her words but he didn't interrupt, just leaned back against the wall, arms folded as she spoke.

'You were very rude to me earlier. You don't know me, and you had no evidence for your words. If it was up to me you would be on your way back to New York right now but for one thing. Your great-aunt. It was her wish that we work together and I intend to honour that. But if you speak to me again the way you did earlier then I will be talking to the solicitors about resigning from the trust.'

She wanted to collapse as she said the words, but forced herself to remain standing and still. Although she couldn't stop her eyes searching his face for telltale signs. For narrowed eyes, a tightened mouth, flaring nostrils. Signs she knew all too well.

She clasped her hands, trying to still their slight tremor. But Max Loveday's face didn't change—except for the dawning hint of respect in his eyes.

'Fair point—or should I say fair points? First of all, please, if we're going to work together, do call me Max. Secondly, I don't live in New York. I live in Connecticut, so if you do send me away please make sure I end up in the correct state. And third…' He paused. 'You're right. I was rude. There are reasons, and they have nothing to do with you. I can only apologise again.' He closed his eyes briefly. 'There are things going on at home that make it hard for me to believe in altruism, and my great-aunt *did* leave you this building.'

'I didn't ask her to.'

'No, but look at it from my point of view. I don't know you. I just see the cold, hard facts. She was on her own…possibly vulnerable. She left her fortune in your—in *our* hands—and bequeathed to *you* a home and livelihood. On paper, that's a little suspicious.'

Ellie hated to admit it, but he had a point—and she had been shocked by the will and her own prominent part in it. There was one thing he hadn't taken into consideration, though.

She laughed. 'You didn't know your great-aunt very well, did you? I can't see her being taken in by *anybody*. She didn't suffer fools gladly.'

'I didn't know her at all. She moved over here before I was born. I wish I'd made an effort to see her before it was too late.'

'You should have done. She was worth knowing. Right, I'm just going to…' She gestured upstairs. 'I won't be long. Make yourself at home.'

She slipped out of the room. She didn't care about impressing Max Loveday, but there was no way she was heading out without brushing her hair and powdering her face. Maybe a quick coat of mascara. To freshen up after a long day at work. That was all.

Trouble was, she wasn't even fooling herself.

So this was Ellie Scott's home. Bright, vibrant, and yet somehow bare. For all the posters on the walls, the cushions heaped on the inviting sofas, the view of the sea from the back window, there was something missing.

Photos. There were no photos. Not on the walls, not on the sideboard, nor on the mantelpiece over the cosy-looking wood-burning stove. He had never yet met a woman who didn't decorate her personal space with family portraits, pictures of friends, holidays, favourite pets, university formals. Max himself had a framed picture of his parents on his desk in his office, and a few childhood photos in his apartment. The picture of himself aged about ten on his grandfather's boat, proudly holding up a large fish, was one of his most prized possessions.

Maybe they were tucked away like her books, but somehow he doubted it. Where had she come from? What had made a young woman in her early twenties move to a tiny village miles from civilisation and stay there? Or had she walked out of the sea? A selkie doomed to spend her life in human form until she found her sealskin once more? With those huge brown eyes and long, long lashes Ellie certainly fitted the bill.

'Okay, ready when you are. I hope I didn't keep you waiting too long?'

When Ellie had said she would be a minute Max had been prepared for a twenty-minute wait. Minimum. Yet barely five minutes had passed since she had left. She had pulled a long light grey cardigan over her tunic, swapped her pumps for sneakers and brushed out her hair. That was it.

Yet she looked completely fresh, like a dryad in spring.

Anything less like the manicured, blow-dried, designer-clad women he worked with, dated and slept with was hard to imagine. But right now she was fresh iced water to their over-sugared and over-carbonated soda. Not that he was looking in any real way. It was the contrast, that was all. It wasn't that he was actually interested in wholesome girls with creamy skin. He just didn't know many. Or *any*.

'Yes. Ready.' He might be staring. He wasn't staring like some gauche teenage boy, was he? Reluctantly he pulled his gaze away. 'Come on, honey, let's go.'

* * *

The sharp breeze that had greeted him earlier in the day had died away, and despite the hour the sun still cast a warm glow over the village. The gentle warmth was a welcome contrast to the heat and humidity of home and the wet and cold of the Sydney winter—not that Sydney's worst could compare to the bone-chilling cold of a Connecticut winter, but it could still be unpleasant.

'There are more houses up there, the school and the children's playground.' Ellie pointed up the hill away from the coast. 'Useful things like the doctor's surgery and the bus stop that takes you to the nearest towns. But I don't suppose you're interested in those?'

'Not unless I was planning to move here.'

'What will you do with the house?' She turned and began to walk the other way, down the hill and towards the swell of the sea. He fell into step beside her.

'I don't know.'

The moment he had stepped into the wide hallway of The Round House, looked at the seascapes and compasses on the walls and heard the rumble of the sea through the windows he had felt a connection. But even the idea of keeping it was impractical.

'It's way too far away to be a holiday home, but now I know there's a real family link I'd hate to sell it on.'

'Trengarth has enough holiday homes. It needs young families to settle here, to put down roots. They're talking about closing down the primary school and bussing the kids over to the next town.' She paused and looked back up the hill. 'Once this was a proper high street: haberdashers, ironmongers, butchers, toy shop…the lot. Your great-aunt has some amazing photos, dating right back to Victorian times. Now it's all gift shops and art galleries, and the front is buckets and spades and surf hire.'

She sounded sad. Nostalgic for a Trengarth she couldn't ever have actually experienced.

'Is that why you moved here? To put down roots?' Was there a family in her future? A man she was hoping to settle down with? There had been no hint of anyone else in her flat. No hint of any family or partner.

'I moved here because it felt safe. Because there was someone here I loved and trusted.'

She didn't say any more, and he didn't push it as they carried on to the bottom of the hill. When they reached it she crossed over the road to a narrow sidewalk, taking the right-hand fork along the harbour wall.

On the other side of the road, houses faced out: brightly coloured terraced cottages in whites, blues, pinks and greens making a cheerful mosaic. Winding narrow streets twisted and turned behind them, with houses built higher and higher up the cliff.

'This is the old town. Most of these would have been fishermen's cottages once.'

'Once?'

'Some still are,' she admitted. 'Some are retirement properties, and a few are owned by villagers. But probably half are holiday cottages. Which is fine when they're full. My business depends on tourists with money to spend and time to browse, and so do the cafés, the B&Bs, the art galleries and the bucket and spade shops. It's when they're empty, or they don't get rented out and are only visited two weeks a year, when it's a problem. That's why it's important that we really try and make this festival a success. It could bring so many more people here.'

She stopped and leaned on the iron railings, looking out over the curve of the old harbour.

'I love this view. The fishing boats safely moored inside the harbour, the powerboats and sailboats further out… Sometimes I wish I could sail, just set off and see where I end up.'

Her voice was unexpectedly wistful. Max stole a glance at her profile. She was in another world, almost oblivious to his presence as she stared out at the white-flecked waves.

'You don't sail? You live by the sea and don't sail? You must surf, then.'

He gave her an appraising look. She was very slim, almost to the point of thin, but there was a strength and a lithe grace in the way she moved. She would probably be a natural on a board.

She shook her head.

'Swim?'

'No.' A reluctant smile curved her mouth. 'I love the sea, but more as something to look at, listen to. I'm not so much one for venturing on to or into it.'

'Wow...' He shook his head. 'You live literally five minutes away and you just *look* at it? I was going to try and hire a boat while I'm here. I think I may have to offer to take you out for a sail. It'll change your life.'

'Maybe.'

It wasn't a refusal, and her smile didn't slip away as she resumed walking.

'Okay, if you take that road there it will lead you to the most important building in Trengarth: The Three Herrings. There *is* another pub further along, with a beer garden and a view of the harbour. It's lovely, but...' She lowered her voice. 'It's mostly used by tourists and incomers. The *real* Trengarthians frequent The Three Herrings, even though there is no view, the chimney smokes and the grub is very much of the plain and plentiful variety.'

'Got it.'

'Do you want to see the beach?'

'Sure.'

They turned around and walked back, past the

high street and onto the wider promenade. No houses here. Just shops selling ice cream, sun cream and beach toys, a couple of board shops filled with body-boards, surfboards and wetsuits, which Max noted with keen interest, and a few cafés.

'The Boat House,' Ellie explained, when he stopped in front of a modern-looking glass and wood building on the ocean side of the road. 'Café by day, bistro by night, and a bit of a cool place to hang out. I used to have dinner with your Great-Aunt Demelza here on a Friday evening.' Her voice softened. 'I turned up as usual the Friday after she died…just automatically, you know? I didn't really take it in that she was gone until I was seated by myself.'

'I'm sorry. Sorry that you miss her and that I didn't know her. And that nobody came to the funeral—although we lost Grandfather just a few months before, and things were difficult.'

That was an understatement. His father had barely finished the eulogy before he'd had started gathering up the reins at DL and turning the company upside down.

'It's okay. Really. I have some experience at arranging funerals.'

There was a bitter note to her voice that surprised him.

'Besides, she was very clear about what she wanted. I didn't have to do much.'

She turned away from The Boat House and headed towards the slipway that would take them on to the beach.

Max stood for one moment to take in the view. The slim figure all in grey was getting smaller as she walked along the wide golden sweep of beach. The cliffs were steeper on this side of the bay, green and yellow with gorse, and rocks and large pebbles were clustered at the bottom before the stony mass gave way to the softer sand.

The sea roared as the tide beat its inexorable way in, the swell significant enough to justify the presence of lifeguards' chairs and warning flags. Not that it seemed to deter the determined crowd of surfers bobbing about like small seals.

The breeze had risen a little. Enough for Max to feel a slight chill on his arms as he stepped on to the sand. He inhaled, enjoying the familiar tang of salt, and heard the cry of gulls overhead and the excited shrieks of a gaggle of small children who were racing a puppy along the tideline.

For the first time in a long time Max could feel the burden on his shoulders slip away, the tightness in his chest ease.

'Hey, Ellie!' he yelled. 'Wait for me.'

He took off after her, enjoying the burn in his calves as he sprinted along the resistant sand, enjoying the complete freedom of the here, the now.

'This is magnificent,' he panted as he skidded to a halt beside her. 'What a beach. If I lived here I'd have two dogs, a boat, and I'd surf every day.'

She flushed. 'I do *walk* on the beach, even if I don't immerse myself in the sea. And I have thought about maybe getting a guinea pig.'

'A *guinea pig*? You can't walk a guinea pig.'

'Some people do. They have harnesses and everything.' But she caught his eye as she said it and a smile broke out on her face: a full-on, wide-mouthed grin.

It transformed her, lighting up the shadows of her face, bringing that elusive prettiness to the forefront. Max stood stock-still, stunned.

'Harnesses...right. I see.' He turned back as he said it, instinctively heading for the safety of the large white house just visible at the top of the cliffs.

He wasn't here to flirt, and Ellie wasn't giving off any signals that she might enjoy the kind of no-strings fun he'd be interested in. It was far better not to notice how her face lit up, not to notice the sparkle in the large eyes or the intriguing dimple in her cheek. Far, *far* better not to notice just how perfectly shaped her mouth was: not too large, not too small, but pretty damn near just right.

'Come on,' he said, bouncing on his heels. 'I'll race you back to the road. Loser buys the winner a pint. Ready? *Go!*'

CHAPTER FOUR

'THAT WASN'T FAIR. You had a head start.' Ellie pulled the long, tangled mass of hair out of her face, twisting it into a loose knot. Her heart was thumping from the unaccustomed exercise. She'd thought she was fitter than that, although she couldn't remember the last time she had run at full pelt, aware of nothing but her legs pumping, her heart beating fit to burst, the wind biting at her ears.

'If you're going to be a sore loser…'

Max looked annoyingly at ease, leaning on the railing and waiting for her, his cheeks unflushed, his chest not heaving for breath. Unlike hers.

'No, no, I concede. I'm not sure I'd have won even with a head start. Next time *I* pick the competition. Speed-reading, maybe.'

She stepped onto the causeway to join him, but as she did so she heard her name called from someone behind her and twisted round to see who it was. It wasn't often she found herself hailed in such a friendly way.

A group of wetsuit-clad surfers had left the sea and were making their way up the beach, boards tucked under their arms.

'Ellie, wait!'

She turned to meet them, all too aware of Max behind her. The surfers were all locals. Some were born and bred, and some were incomers like Ellie, lured to Trengarth by the sea, the scenery and the pace of life. Ellie often forgot just how many people her own age lived in the village, many working at The Boat House café or the hotel of the same name, others owning businesses they ran from their homes. The group in front of her included a talented chef, a website designer and an architect.

'Hi…' She wasn't sure why she was so self-conscious as she called back, but the heat in her cheeks wasn't completely down to her recent exercise.

'Are you coming to the quiz tonight?' asked Sam, the architect, as he jogged ahead of his friends to join her. 'We would never have won last week without you.'

It wasn't often she ventured out, but a week ago she had popped into the pub, completely unaware that it was the weekly hotly contested quiz night, and had been co-opted on to a team. She had felt unexpectedly welcome, and for the first time had been uneasily aware that her incomer status might be something she enforced on herself. Especially where the under-thirties in the village were concerned.

'Well, if you ever picked up a book you might have a chance. I sell quite a selection, you know. Come in and I'll make a personal recommendation.'

'Tempting…' Sam was standing a little closer, his blue eyes smiling down into hers in unmistakable invitation.

Ellie waited for that same jolt of libido she had experienced earlier. Sam was tall, handsome, he wore the tight-fitting wetsuit very well and was looking down at her with appreciation. But, no. Nothing. Not even a tiny electric shock.

Disappointing. He would be a much more suitable person to have a crush on. If only her body would agree.

She took a step back, breaking the connection. 'Besides, I was more than useless at the sports questions and I had no idea how terrible my geography was until last week. I've been paying extra attention when I shelve the travel guides to try and brush up a little.'

'So you'll come?'

The rest of the group had caught up with Sam and were waiting for her answer. She knew them all, but none of them was close enough to count as a friend.

She hadn't noticed the difference before.

'I...I might,' she said finally. 'I was about to pop down to the Herrings to introduce Max to the place so... Oh, this is Max Loveday. Miss Loveday's great-nephew. He's come over to sort out the house and help me make a start on the festival.'

She was aware of Sam's appraising gaze as she introduced the rest of the group to Max, and was glad when she could finally make her escape with the promise that she might see them later.

Max didn't speak for a few moments as they retraced their steps along the seafront, but the silence was tight, the easy camaraderie of the beach gone as if it had never been.

'Is he your boyfriend?'

Ellie felt her cheeks warm again. She didn't need to ask who he was referring to. 'No.' She was glad her voice didn't squeak. 'I'm not seeing anyone at the moment. Are you?'

What did they say? Attack was the best form of defence, and she really didn't want to be discussing her personal life with anyone. Especially not with Max Loveday.

'Me?' His voice was amused. 'Not at the moment. My last relationship ended a couple of months ago. I was always too busy to date, and it was apparent that our timetables didn't match, so I called it off.'

He sounded as detached as if he were discussing cancelling a dinner reservation, not ending an intimate relationship.

'Your *timetables*?' Had she misheard? Was that some kind of slang term for sexual compatibility? Or something really hip to do with auras?

'Stella wanted to get engaged this year, but I'm not going to get married before thirty. Ideally I would like to be around thirty-four, and I don't really want to think about kids until two years after that.' He shrugged as if that was the most natural reason to break up in the world.

'But...' She stared at his profile in fascination, looking for some hint that he was teasing her. 'Didn't you love her?'

'I liked her. We had a lot in common. She was from my world.' Max paused. 'That's what's important. That's what ensures a harmonious marriage. Love isn't enough of a bedrock to build a marriage, a family on. It's not solid enough, not real enough.'

'It isn't? Surely it's the most important thing?'

Despite her hideous three years with Simon and his warped idea of what love meant, in spite of her mother's inability to exist without it, love was still the goal. Wasn't it? Right now she might only find it in books and films, but one day, when her libido was behaving itself and she found herself attracted to the right man at the right time, she hoped she would fall in love. Properly this time. Not mistaking infatuation and fear for the real thing.

She hadn't even considered a timetable.

'My parents were madly in love.' His mouth twisted. '*Madly* being the operative word. Apart from the times when my father was in love with someone else. I don't know which was worse: the awful strained silences, the lies and the falsity when he was having an affair, or the making up afterwards. Once he bought my mother a Porsche. Red, of course. Filled it with one thousand red roses and heart-shaped balloons.'

'Oh, that sounds…' Ellie fought to find the right word and failed.

'Vulgar?' His voice was grim. 'It was. I don't want that kind of ridiculous drama in my life. Respect and mutual goals are a far tidier way to live. A lot less destructive.'

'My parents loved each other too.' The familiar lump rose in her throat at the memory. 'But there was no drama. They were just really happy.'

Max stared straight ahead. 'I spent most of my childhood either playing peacekeeper and go-between or being ignored as they went off on yet another honeymoon. Unless I was with my grandfather. It was all much more stable there.'

'Sounds like he wasn't so different from your Great-Aunt Demelza. She was one of the calmest people I knew.'

'Mmm...'

His mind was clearly elsewhere.

'Ellie, would you mind if I took a raincheck on the pint? I'm still pretty jetlagged and it's been a long few days. But tomorrow I'm going to start going through the house and I would really appreciate your help. You knew her best.'

'Of course.'

Ellie was relieved not to have to spend more time with him now. Especially not in the intimate setting of The Three Herrings, where the little cubicle-like snugs meant an easy drink could easily feel like a *tête-à-tête*. And it meant she could definitely get out of the pub quiz and curl up with her book, just as she had planned.

Yes, she was definitely relieved. She wasn't feeling a little flat at all...

For the longest time The Round House had been the place that Ellie loved best in all the world. It wasn't just its curious shape, like something out of a fairytale, with its high circular roof, the huge arched windows looking out to sea. Nor was it just the knowledge that in its rounded walls were rooms full of treasures. Whether your tastes ran to books, clothes, jewellery, home-baked food or collections of everything from stamps to fossils, somewhere in the various cupboards, cabinets and boxes there was bound to be something to catch your eye.

Once, at first, it had been her holiday home: the flagstone hallway liberally sprinkled with sand as she ran in straight from the beach, barely pausing to wrap a towel around her before heading to the kitchen for freshly baked scones and a glass of creamy Cornish milk. Later it had been a place for grief and contemplation, long hours huddled in the window seat on the first-floor landing, staring out to sea, wondering just where it was she belonged.

And then it had been a refuge. Literally. A place to regroup, to lick her wounds. Demelza Loveday had given her all the time, space and love in the world. It was a debt she could never repay. Making sure she helped her godmother's dream of a literary festival come true was the least she could do.

But today, watching Max open the arched front door and invite her in, a realisation hit her. One she hadn't allowed herself to articulate before.

The Round House would never be her home again. It belonged to Max Loveday. From now on it would be a second home, visited once a year, or sold on to strangers. Her last link to Demelza Loveday would be severed.

But for the moment at least nothing had changed. The hallway was still furnished with the same aged elegance; the glass bowl on the sideboard was set in the same position. Only the hat stand was missing its usual mackintosh and scarf. Demelza's clothes had long since been gathered up and given away to charity.

'Is something wrong?'

Ellie started, aware that she had been standing immobile, staring around the hallway for far too long. 'No, sorry. It's just...' She hesitated, unsure how to articulate the strange sense of wrongness. Then it came to her. 'It smells all wrong.'

Max sniffed. 'It was a little musty when I got here, I've had all the windows open, though.'

'No, it's not that.' It wasn't what she could smell, more what she couldn't. That elusive sense that something important was missing. 'There's no smell of baking. No perfume in the air. Your great-aunt liked a very floral scent, quite heavy. It's gone now.'

Max leaned back against the wall, his casual stance and clothes incongruous against the daintily patterned wallpaper. 'The whole house was cleaned after her clothes were disposed of—she'd asked that they were given away or sold, and I guess the executors took care of that. But all her papers are here. Her books, pictures, ornaments. I have no idea what to do with it all.'

He didn't sound dismissive. Not exactly. But nor did he sound at all appreciative. He had no idea how special his gift was.

'Where do you want to start?' It wasn't his fault, Ellie reminded herself. He didn't have the links she did. What were treasured memories to her must just be so much clutter to him.

'In the library. The solicitor gave me the key

to her desk. Apparently all the papers in there are mine now. They sold off the stocks and other financial assets for the trust so it must all be family stuff.'

'More information about the sea captain?'

The pinched expression left his face. 'Maybe. That would be cool.'

In Ellie's admittedly not at all unbiased opinion, the library was the heart of the house. Demelza had turned what had been the morning room into a book-lined paradise filled with window seats and cosy nooks. In summer you could look out upon the ocean, basking in the sun through the open French windows; in winter a roaring fire warmed you as you read. The rounded walls held glassed-in bookshelves, reaching from floor to ceiling. Polished oak floorboards were covered with vibrant rugs in turquoises and emeralds. The same colours were reflected in the curtains and the geometric Art Deco wallpaper.

Would whoever bought this house keep the room this way? It was horribly unlikely.

Max had wandered over to the far side of the room, where he was examining a case of blue-bound hardbacks. 'She owned the entire catalogue…' His voice was reverential. 'That's incredible.'

'I was only allowed to touch those under strict supervision even when I was all grown up. She said they had too much sentimental value.'

Max raised an eyebrow. 'Not just sentimental; they're worth a *fortune* to collectors. These are all first edition Kerenza Press classics.' He opened the glass door and carefully slid one out. 'Just look at the quality…the illustrations. We stopped producing these years ago. I always wished we had carried on.'

'We?'

'DL Media. Kerenza was the very first imprint my great-grandfather started. He named it after his wife, my great-grandmother.' His mouth twisted. 'It means "love" in Cornish.'

'It's a beautiful name.' No wonder Demelza had such an amazing collection of books, but why had she never mentioned that she was part of the DL Media empire? All those long talks about books, about the shop, about the festival, and she had never once let slip her literary heritage.

For the first time Ellie was conscious of a gap between her godmother and herself. Not of age, or privilege, but of secrets withheld, confidences untold.

'I knew that you worked for DL Media because of your email. I didn't know that you *were* DL.'

Ellie gave a little laugh, but it sounded false even to her own ears. Max was heir to one of the last big publishing and media companies in private hands. No wonder he wore an air of wealth and privilege like a worn-in sweatshirt: so comfortable it was almost part of him.

'She didn't mention it?'

Ellie shook her head. 'Never. She never really spoke about her life in America. Sometimes she would talk about her university days here in England. That's how she knew my grandmother. All she said about her working life was that she regretted never marrying but that in her day women could have jobs or they could have marriage, not both. She never mentioned her family or *where* she'd worked.'

'She worked for DL until my great-grandfather died. Then there was some kind of argument—

about the will and the direction of the company, I think.' His face was set as he stared at the book in his hands. 'There's nothing to tear a family apart like money. Wills and family businesses must be responsible for more fractures than anything else.'

'Oh, I don't know…' That old bone-deep ache pulsed. 'Families fracture for many reasons. But sometimes we forge our own family ties. Blood doesn't always run deeper.'

'You're not close to your family?'

'I lost my father and brother in a car accident.' How could something so utterly destructive be explained in just a few words? How could the ripping apart of a family be distilled down to one sentence? 'My mother remarried.'

'I'm so sorry.' His eyes had darkened with sympathy, the expression in them touching somewhere buried deep inside her, warming, defrosting. But the barriers were there for a reason.

She stepped back, putting even more space between them. 'It was a long time ago.'

'Do you like your stepfather?'

'He makes my mother happy. She's not really

the kind of person who copes well by herself. It's a relief to know that someone is taking care of her.'

It was the truth, so why did it feel as if she were lying?

'I'll definitely ship all this back, but nothing seems urgent.' Max stared at the floor of the library, now liberally covered in papers, paperclips and folders.

His great-aunt had definitely been a hoarder. And an avid family historian. There was enough here to write a biography of the entire Loveday clan—one with several volumes. But so far he hadn't found anything to indicate that she had still owned part of the company.

Ellie sat cross-legged close by, sorting through some of the newer-looking files, many of which were about village committees and his great-aunt's charitable commitments.

'This looks different. It's in a legal envelope and addressed to you, so I haven't opened it.' Ellie handed over a large manila envelope. His name was neatly typed on the label.

‘Thanks…’

This could be it. His pulse began to speed as he reached for the envelope, and then accelerated as his hand brushed hers. His fingers wanted to latch on to hers, keep holding on. Her hair had fallen out of its clip while they worked and she had allowed it to flow free. Max could barely keep his eyes off the smooth flow of hair, constantly changing colour in the sunlit room, one moment dark chocolate, the next a rich bronze.

It had to be natural. He couldn’t imagine Ellie sitting for hours in a hairdresser’s chair. His mother had her hair cut and dyed monthly, at a salon that charged the equivalent of a month’s rent for the privilege.

No wonder her alimony demands were so high.

‘What is it? A treasure map for some ancient pirate Loveday’s plunder?’

‘Fingers crossed.’ If it was what he was hoping for then it would be worth far more than any treasure chest.

Max slit the envelope open and pulled out a single sheet of paper.

‘No X marks the spot.’

'Disappointing.' Ellie got to her feet in one graceful gesture. 'Shall I start tidying some of this lot up? I don't think there's any way you're going to get through this entire house in just two weeks.'

He could barely make out her words. All his attention was on the piece of paper he held. 'Read this. What does it say?'

She glanced at him, puzzled, before taking the paper. Max rocked back on his heels, his blood pumping so loudly he could barely make out her voice as she read the paper aloud.

'It says that Demelza remained a silent shareholder even after her severance from DL Media and that she's left her twenty-five per cent share of the company to you. Very nice.'

Yes! This was it. He quickly totted up the percentages in his mind.

'More than nice.' He was on his feet, his hand on hers where she held the precious paper. 'It means my grandfather only held seventy-five per cent of the company. And *that* means my father doesn't have a two-thirds majority. We're equal partners. Do you know what else, Ellie Scott? It means I can take him on and I can *win*. Thanks to my lovely Great-Aunt Demelza.'

'It does?' She was staring up at him, smiling in response, her eyes enormous, her cheeks flushed.

The breath whooshed from his chest as if he had been hit with a football at top speed. How did she do it? How did that elusive smile light her up, turn the pointed chin, big eyes and hollow cheeks into beauty?

And why didn't she smile more often?

Max took a deep breath, curling his fingers into his palms. All he wanted to do was touch her, trace the curve of her cheek, run a finger along the fullness of her bottom lip and tangle his hands in the thick length of hair. But he knew instinctively, with every bone in his body, that his touch would be unwelcome. There was a 'Keep Out' sign erected very firmly around Ellie. Trespassers were most certainly not tolerated.

She would have to invite him in. And he sensed that invitations were very rarely issued, if at all.

It was for the best. A girl like Ellie didn't know how to play. She would need wooing and loving and protecting. All the things he had no interest in.

She stepped back, leaving the precious paper in his hands. 'You and your father are disagreeing?'

That was one way of putting it.

Max walked over to the window and stared out at the breathtaking view. The Round House was at the very top of the cliff. Just a few metres of garden seemed to separate the house from the sea stretching out to the horizon beyond.

'My grandfather was a visionary. He was an early adopter of technology, but managed to avoid the dotcom crisis, and we've weathered every financial crisis there's been. My father was always in his shadow, I guess. But since Grandfather died he's seemed determined to put his stamp on the company. He thinks anything new is worth investing in, and he's diversifying the brand into everything from jobs to dating. If there's an app for it he wants it.'

Ellie stepped forward and stood next to him, so close they were almost touching. *Almost.* 'Most media outlets have job sites and dating adverts…'

'Supported by their main publications, they can

be useful income streams, yes.' He ran a hand through his hair. 'But he's not investing in the news sites at all. He's got rid of some of our most experienced journalists and is allowing bloggers and the commenting public to provide most of the content. There's a place for that, sure, but not at the expense of your main news. I came here to find a way to wrestle control of the company away from him. This—' he brandished the paper '—this means we either come to a consensus or every decision goes to the board. It's not ideal, but it's a helluva lot better than the current situation.'

'It sounds like your grandfather and your great-aunt all over again.'

He flinched at her gentle words. Was she right? Was another massive chasm about to open up in the family?

'It's not just work.' He was justifying his actions as much to himself as he was to Ellie. 'His personal life is a mess too. He's left my mother for my old PA, and just to twist the cliché has announced he wants a divorce.'

He couldn't talk about the pregnancy. Not yet.

'My mother is a mess, *he* is completely unrepentant, and DL Media is fragmenting. I have a lot of work to do.'

'Max, they're grown-ups. Isn't their marriage *their* problem? Getting sucked in too far never ends well.' There was a bitter certainty in her voice.

Max laughed, the anger in the sound startling him. 'Oh, their marriage *is* their problem. I'm not getting involved. Not any more. But I have to look after DL, whatever it takes. My mother is out for blood. She wants half the company. Can you imagine? The lawyers' fees alone could drag us down.'

'What would happen if you just walked away? They'd have to fix it then, wouldn't they?'

He shook his head. 'It's not so much them as the company. It's *my* responsibility, Ellie. I started in the distribution centre when I was fifteen. I was filing and photocopying at sixteen, writing up press releases at eighteen. I interned every year I was at Yale, and when I graduated I went straight into the New Media department. It's all I've ever known and I *won't* let them tear it apart.'

'I always wanted to work in publishing.' There was a longing in her voice. 'But I didn't go to university.'

'Why not?' It was a relief to change the subject, to focus on something else.

'My mother took a long time to get over my father's death. It was hard to leave her. And when she remarried I was…' She swallowed, her already pale cheeks whitening. 'I was engaged.'

'You were *engaged*?' He turned to look at her, shocked by her revelation. She was very pale. Even her lips were almost white.

'Yes. I was young and foolish and had no judgement.'

She smiled at him but he wasn't fooled. This smile didn't light up her face, didn't illuminate her beauty. It was only skin-deep, false.

The urge to protect her swept up, taking him completely by surprise. Somehow he knew, completely and utterly, that Ellie Scott had been badly hurt and that the scars were still not fully healed. Another reason to keep well away.

'It's not too late.'

'I'm doing a degree now, in the evenings. And

at least I'm surrounded by books. It's not all bad. But what would you do if you weren't part of DL? If you weren't one of *those* Lovedays?'

But he *was* one of 'those' Lovedays. His identity was burnt into him like a brand. He couldn't escape his family history and nor did he want to.

'All I ever wanted was to make my grandfather proud and take DL to the next level.' It didn't sound like much, but it was everything. 'I can't let my father stop that.'

'Can't you work *with* him? Compromise?'

'He won't let me in, Ellie. I've tried, goodness knows. He wants me to knuckle down and accept him as head of the family. To tamely agree with every decision he makes, to meet the woman he's left my mother for and make her part of my family. We can't even be in the same room right now.'

'Then it's a good thing you're on the other side of the Atlantic.'

Max caught sight of his reflection in the mirror on the wall opposite, jaw set, eyes hard. He barely recognised himself.

'Maybe.' He made an effort to shake off the anger coiling around his soul like a malevolent snake. 'I need to get this faxed over to the company lawyers before I go to London. I can plan my next move from there. I'll get someone in to clear the rest of the house before I instruct the solicitors to sell.'

'You're not thinking of keeping the house?' Disappointment flickered over her face. 'Your Great-Aunt Demelza would have wanted you to.'

'My life's in Connecticut. When I'm in the UK I'm London-based. I have no use for it.'

Looking around, he felt a hint of regret. His family's history was soaked into the rounded walls. His eyes fell on a gilt-edged card as he spoke. It looked familiar and, curious, he picked it up.

'What's this?'

Ellie flushed and reached for it. Max held it a little longer, trying to read the curled writing, until with a pull she tugged it out of his fingers. 'Oh, that's mine. It must have fallen out of my bag. It's just some industry black tie thing. I've been nominated for Independent Bookseller of the Year. Nonsense, really, but quite sweet.'

'Are you going?'

'Oh, no. It's in London. The season starts this week. I couldn't leave the shop. Besides, I wouldn't know anyone.'

Max reached over and plucked the card out of her hand. Why was it striking a chord?

'DL have a table.'

That was it. The London office had asked him to attend and it would be the perfect opportunity for him to quell some of the rumours about the company's viability.

'You could come with me. That way you wouldn't be going alone.'

Her face turned even redder. 'That's very kind of you…'

'Not at all. I hate these things. It would be more bearable if I was with someone I knew. Especially if that someone was up for an award.'

'There's still the shop…'

'Mrs Trelawney is quite capable, surely? Look, Ellie, I was planning on going anyway. It would make me very happy if you came with me.'

Max didn't know why it mattered. She was a grown woman…she could do as she pleased. But although black tie dinners and awards ceremonies were a dime a dozen to him, he sensed they didn't really figure in Ellie's life. Besides, his great-aunt had loved Ellie, cared for her. It would be fitting thanks if he took her under his wing a little.

In fact he was being very altruistic.

'I appreciate the thought…'

'I'm not doing this to be kind,' he reassured her. 'My motives are completely selfish.'

'I really wasn't planning on going.'

'If we are going to be setting up a literary festival then this is the best thing you can do. I'll introduce you to some of the best publicists in the business. And who knows, Ellie? We might even have fun while we're there.'

CHAPTER FIVE

ELLIE DIDN'T ACTUALLY remember agreeing to *any* of this.

Not to going to the awards ceremony and certainly not to spending two nights in London with someone she barely knew.

She'd spent far too long allowing her wishes to be overridden, doing things she didn't want to in order to placate someone else: three years indulging her mother's grief, three years trying to turn herself into the perfect wife for Simon. Both had been impossible tasks.

She'd sworn she'd never allow herself to be pushed out of her comfort zone. Not ever again.

So why was she now sitting in the passenger seat of Max Loveday's hire car, watching the miles disappear as London grew ever closer?

The thing was, she couldn't deny a certain fizz in her veins, a delicious anticipation. It was mixed with fear and dread, yes, but it was anticipation nonetheless.

After three years of living very much within her comfort zone she was ready to be stretched, just a little. And if she must be stretched then a champagne reception seemed like a reasonable place to start. It wasn't as if she was going to *win* the award. All she had to do was smile and applaud the winner.

And start to make contacts for the festival. That was a little more daunting. But Max must know the right people. He could take care of that, surely?

'Penny for them?'

'I'm sorry?'

'For your thoughts. You've been pretty quiet the whole journey. I can hear the wheels turning.'

Ellie sank back in the admittedly plush seat and stared out at the countryside. The harsh beauty of the Cornish moors had given way first to rolling hills and now to pastoral scenes fit for a movie. Sheep grazed in fields dotted by small lines of trees; copses dominated the skyline in the distance. At any moment she expected to pass through idyllic villages full of thatched cottages and maypoles.

Ellie bit her lip. It was odd, this new companionship. She'd spent more time in the last few days with Max Loveday than she had with any other person in the entire last three years—other than Demelza Loveday, of course. That must be why, despite his complete and utter lack of suitability, she found herself wanting to confide in him.

Besides, a little voice whispered, he had confided in *her.* She'd seen a crack in his façade—and she'd liked what she'd seen. Someone who wasn't *quite* so certain of his place in the world. Someone with questions. He was ruthless, sure, and ready to sacrifice his father if need be—not for personal gain, but because he genuinely believed it would be for the best. That took a lot of strength.

'This is the first time I've left Trengarth in three years.'

He darted a look over at her. 'Seriously?'

Ellie nodded.

Max let out a low whistle. 'What are you?

Twenty-five? Trengarth is pretty, but that's kinda young to be burying yourself away.'

'I didn't even realise that was what I was doing. I feel…' She hesitated, searching for the right word, not wanting to reveal too much. '*Safe* there.'

'You haven't even visited your mom?'

There was a particular ache that squeezed Ellie's chest whenever she thought about her mother: a toxic mixture of hurt and regret and a deep sense of loss.

'She's so busy, and she and my stepfather travel a great deal. Not to Cornwall, though,' she couldn't help adding, wincing at the acidity in her voice. 'But it's good to get away. Even for a couple of days. When we drove out of the village I felt as if I was leaving a cage—a little scared, but free.'

Whoa! That was far too revealing. She peeped over at Max, but his face was smoothly bland.

'Sometimes we need the perspective we get just by being in a new place.'

'I think maybe this festival is what I need. Perhaps I have got a little…' She paused, searching for the right word. 'Comfortable. After all, I host signings and launches, book clubs and children's activities. It's just a case of combining them all.'

'You'll be great.'

Would she? It was so long since she'd struck out, dared to dream of anything but safety, a bolt-hole of her own.

That was what Simon had taken from her. Not just her confidence and her self-esteem but also her time. Three years with him. Three years recovering from him. Time she could never get back.

Maybe all this was a sign. Max, the bequest, the award nomination. A big neon sign, telling her she needed to stop being afraid. That she had to go out there and live.

'Once I thought I'd live in London. That I'd have a flat, go to plays in the evenings, wander around exhibitions at lunchtime. Sometimes I feel like I skipped a stage in my life. Headed right for settling down and forgot to have the fun bit first.'

Ellie risked a look over at Max.

His face was bleak. 'You and me both.'

The traffic thickened as they got closer to London, the green fields giving way to buildings and warehouses.

'Why?'

She started, the one-word question rousing her from her thoughts. 'Why what?'

'Why did you hide away?'

His words hit her with an almost physical force, winding her so that for one never-ending moment she was breathless. *Why?* Because she had allowed herself to be used and manipulated for so long that she hadn't known who she was any more. But how could she say those words out loud even to herself—let alone to the confident, successful man beside her?

He might understand a little how she had been trapped by her mother's need and grief, forced to grow up too soon, to make sure that bills were paid and food was on the table and that somehow the half of her family that was left survived. Yes, he would understand that.

But would he understand her later weakness—or despise her for it? Heaven knew she despised herself. Max Loveday had made it quite clear that he thought love was a lie, an emotional trap.

What would he think of a lonely girl so desperate for affection and for someone to take care of her that she'd fallen prey to a controlling relationship, allowed her soul to be stripped bare until she had no idea who she was, what she wanted?

How could he understand it when she didn't understand it herself? It was her shame, her burden.

'I don't want to talk about Trengarth. I haven't been to London for ages. What shall we do there?'

He shot her an amused smile. 'Work, go to a party...the usual.'

She seized on the statement, glad of the change of topic. 'You've been in Cornwall for four days and in that time you've spent half the day on paperwork and the rest of the day and evening working. You make noises about sailing and surfing, but you haven't left the house long enough to do either.'

Irritation scratched through his voice. 'This isn't a holiday, Ellie.'

'No,' she said sweetly. 'It *is* the weekend, though. And as you have somehow talked me into a few days away I, for one, am planning to do some sightseeing. I'll take photos for you, shall I?'

'Okay.'

'Okay to photos?'

He sighed. 'No. Okay to the rest of the weekend off. You're right. I'm nearly halfway through this trip and I haven't stopped. We should have fun in London. Let's be tourists. For today at least.'

We? A warmth stole over her. Ellie had spent so long keeping people at arm's length that although she had plenty of cordial acquaintances she wasn't at the top of very many people's 'going out' lists.

But Max Loveday wanted to go out and have fun. With her.

'Be tourists?' she echoed. 'Like the Houses of Parliament and Buckingham Palace?'

'Like all the big sights. No work and no cares this afternoon or this evening, Heck. I might even take tomorrow off too, before we have to dress up for this award nonsense. But for today we forget about bequests and festivals and DL Media. We're just two people out and about. Just two people in the city. What do you think?'

What did she think? He wanted to spend time with her, he wanted to know what her opinion was, he wanted just to hang out. With her. To have a day of carefree, irresponsible, forget-your-worries fun.

When had Ellie *ever* had a day like that? Goodness, she was pathetic. Max was right. Didn't she deserve a day out of time?

Before she forgot how to let go at all.

'I think we should do it. Where do you want to go?' She pulled her phone out, ready to search the internet.

'Let's not plan. Let's just go for it and see where we end up.'

Ellie took in a deep breath, damping down the knot of worry forming in her stomach. She could do this. She didn't need to plan everything. Spontaneous. Fun. Those adjectives *could* describe her.

They had once described the little girl running barefoot through the sand at Trengarth, living completely and utterly in the moment. She was still in there somewhere. Wasn't she?

'Perfect. We'll see where we end up. Absolutely.'

* * *

Max seemed to take the hotel completely in his stride, but although Ellie wanted to look like the kind of girl who stayed in sumptuous five-star hotels every day of her life she was aware she was failing miserably, gaping at everything from the uniformed doorman to the gilt-edged baroque decorations.

'I don't think this is within my budget,' she whispered to Max as the doorman took her case, not betraying with so much as a flicker of his eyebrow that her old tattered holdall was easily the cheapest item in the entire hotel.

She'd known they were going to stay somewhere nice, had justified the extravagance as a business expense, but this? This was the difference between high street chocolate and handmade truffles.

It wasn't just nice, and *luxurious* didn't come close. It was the *haute couture* of the hotel world. And Ellie was very much a high street girl.

She cast a surreptitious look around, trying to find some clue as to the tariff. But there was nothing. *If you have to ask the price you can't afford it...* Wasn't that what they said?

What if you were terrified to ask the price? That meant you absolutely couldn't afford so much as a sandwich in the lavishly decorated bar.

It wasn't as if she spent much, but one night in this hotel might severely deplete her carefully hoarded savings. Her nails bit into her palms as she fought for breath. She didn't have to stay. She could go and find a more affordable room right now.

Only the doorman had shepherded them into the lift and the doors were beginning to close. Would it be too late when he opened the door to her room? It might be okay... If she bought sandwiches from a shop down the road and didn't go anywhere near the mini-bar...

And there was always her emergency credit card. Her breath hitched. She should be glad that an emergency had been downgraded from an escape plan to paying for a luxury hotel room.

'Relax, this is on DL Media,' Max whispered back.

How had he done that? Read her mood so effortlessly?

Relief warred with panic. She *always* paid her way. Money had been just one of the ways Simon had liked to control her. One of the ways she had allowed him to control her.

'Don't be silly. Of course I'll pay my own bill.'

Max leaned in closer and his eyes held hers for a long moment before hers fell under his scrutiny. But that was no better, because now she was staring intently at the grey cotton of his T-shirt where it moulded to his chest.

It was fair to say, Ellie had conceded in the sleepless depths of the night before, that Max Loveday was a reasonably attractive male. He was young, fit, intelligent, and he had that certain air of unconscious arrogance. Infuriating and yet with a certain charm.

But had she *really* noticed? Had she taken the time before now to appreciate the toned strength of him, the long muscled legs, today casually clad in worn jeans, the flat stomach and broad chest? Of course they had never been in quite such close proximity before. She hadn't allowed him within real touching distance.

They weren't touching now, but there were mere millimetres between their bodies. His breath was cool on her cheek and his outdoorsy scent of salt air and pine was enfolding her as every inch of her began to sense every inch of him. An ache began to pulse low in the very centre of her.

He leaned in a millimetre further. 'DL Media pays for the hotel. You get dinner tonight. Deal?'

A compromise. Sensible, fair; no games, no coercion. The ache intensified, spreading upwards, downwards, everywhere. Her pulse speeded up. She wanted to lean in, to allow herself to feel him, touch him.

'Deal.' Ellie could hardly form the word. Her throat was dry. There was no air in this lift, no air at all.

At which point had she begun to notice him? Learned the way his hair curled despite its short cut trying to subdue it into businesslike submission? Learned the line of his jaw and the way his mouth curled sometimes in impatience, sometimes in disdain. sometimes in humour? Learned the gleam in the light brown eyes and the way they could focus on a person as if seeing right into their core?

How had she learned him by heart when she had been trying so hard not to see him at all?

Ellie took a step back, perspiration beading her forehead as the temperature in the suddenly too small lift rocketed. Could he tell? Could he tell that she was horrifyingly, intensely burning up with unwanted attraction? Not that it had that much to do with him *per se*. It had everything to do with three years of celibacy, emotional as well as physical.

She wasn't superficial enough to fall for a lazy smile and an air of entitlement. Oh, no. She had been blinded by charm once. She was just ready to move on, that was all. And he was a temporary fixture in her life. Safe. A two-week stopgap. That was why he was the perfect person to hack through the forest and reawaken those long-dormant feelings.

Only he didn't feel quite so safe now.

'This way please, sir…madam.'

Thank goodness. The lift doors were open and

there was her escape. A hotel room came with a bathroom, which meant one thing: a long and very cold shower. And forget all those good intentions regarding the mini-bar, Ellie needed a large glass of wine and chocolate and she didn't much care which came first.

And then she would give herself a very stern talking-to indeed.

Max stood back to let Ellie precede him out of the lift and she resisted the urge—barely—to press herself against the opposite side of the door and keep as much space between them as possible. He fell in behind her and she stiffened, all too aware of his step matching hers.

Cold shower, wine, chocolate, stern words.

Or maybe stern words, wine, cold shower, chocolate.

And a plan. A plan to start dating. There were single men in Trengarth. Sam was interested, she was almost sure of that, and there were more eligible bachelors. She would find them. She would track them down and she would have coffee and conversation just like any girl of twenty-five ought to.

Maybe even a stroll on a beach, if she was feeling daring.

'Madam, sir…this way, please.' The doorman opened a door and stood aside, an expectant look on his face.

Only it was one door.

One. Door.

Ellie stopped still.

'Madam?' There was a puzzled note in the smooth tones. 'The Presidential Suite…'

Ellie tried to speak. 'I…' Nope, that was more of a squeak. She coughed. 'Suite?' Still a squeak, but a discernible one.

There was a smothered sound from behind her and she narrowed her eyes. If Max Loveday was laughing at her then he was in for a very painful sobering up.

'Yes, madam, our very best suite. As requested.'

Ellie swivelled and fixed the openly grinning Max with her best gimlet glare. 'Suite?'

'My very efficient PA. She must have assumed…' He trailed off, but didn't seem in the least bit repentant. 'Chill, honey. I'm sure that the suite is plenty big enough, and if not I'll find you a broom cupboard somewhere.'

'I'm afraid the hotel is fully booked, sir.' The doorman didn't sound in the least bit sorry. 'If you would like to follow me?'

Stay in the corridor and sulk? Retrieve her bag from the doorman and head out into London to find a new hotel within her budget? Or walk into the suite like an aristocrat headed for the guillotine?

The tumbril it was.

On the one hand it was pretty demoralising to see just how much Ellie Scott *didn't* want to share a hotel suite with him. It wasn't that Max had expected or particularly wanted to share a room with her, but he hadn't faced the prospect with all the icy despair of one prepared to Meet Her Doom.

Plus, he wasn't *that* terrible a prospect. All his own hair, heir to one of the biggest family businesses in the world, reasonably fit and able to string a few sentences together. In some quarters he was quite the catch. But Ellie's ill-hidden horror burst any ego bubble with a resounding bang.

Although it *was* amusing to watch her torn between her obvious dismay at his proximity and her even more obvious open-mouthed appreciation of the lavishly appointed suite.

Goodness knew what Lydia, his PA, was thinking. She usually booked him into business hotels. More than comfortable, certainly, equipped with twenty-four-hour gyms, generous desk space and the kind of comprehensive room service menu that a man heading from meeting to meeting required. A world away from *this* boutique luxury.

This suite took comfort to a whole new level. It didn't say *business*, instead it screamed *honeymoon*—or *dirty weekend.* From the huge bath, more than big enough for two, to the fine linen sheets on the massive bed the suite was all about staying in.

Luckily for Ellie's blood pressure, it also came with a second bedroom. The bed there was a mere super-king-size, and the bathroom came with a walk in shower and a normal-sized bath—but the large sitting and dining area separated the two, and Ellie had claimed the smaller of the two rooms in a way that had made it very clear that trespassers were most definitely not allowed.

And in the hour since they had first entered the suite she had clammed up in a way that showed just how discombobulated she was. Even now, walking down the wide bustling street, she was pale and silent. And it didn't matter, it shouldn't matter, but Max had quite liked the way she had opened up earlier.

The way *he* had opened up.

It had almost been as if they were friends. And it was only with the resounding sound of her silence that he'd realised just how few of those he had. Buddies? Sure. Lovers? Absolutely. Colleagues, teammates, old school and college alumni, relatives, people he'd grown up with—his life was filled with people.

But how many of them were real *friends*? He hadn't discussed his parents' bitter divorce, his doubts about his father's helming of the company with anyone. Not with a single soul.

And yet he'd unburdened himself to this slim, serious English girl.

If she froze him out now then he would be back to where he had started. Dealing with feelings that were seared into his soul, struggling to keep them under control.

Besides, it would be a long two days if she was going to make monosyllabic seem chatty.

Which tactic? Normally he would try and make her laugh. Keep up a flow of light-hearted jokes until she smiled. It was the way he had always dealt with frowns and stony silences.

And if that didn't work then he would walk away without a backward glance. After all, life was too short for emotional manipulation, wasn't it?

But somehow he didn't think that she was trying to manipulate him—nor that a quip would work here. And he was honour-bound to stay. It might be time to dig out honesty…

'I didn't plan to share a suite with you. I hope you know that?'

Ellie stopped abruptly, ignoring the muttered curses of the tourists and business folk who had to skirt around her. 'I *don't* know that. I don't know you well enough.'

'I hope you know me well enough to acknowledge that I would never be sleazy enough to go for the "accidentally booked one room" trick. I don't use tricks, Ellie. If I wanted you to share my bed I'd tell you—and you would have every opportunity to turn me down with no hard feelings.'

She looked hard at him, as if she were trying to learn his every flaw, as if she were burrowing deep into the heart of him. He tried not to squirm—what would she find there? A hollowness? A shallowness?

'Okay.' She started walking again.

'Okay?' *That was all?*

'I'm sorry I doubted you.' Her voice quietened and she looked straight ahead. He got the feeling she was avoiding his eye. 'My...my ex was all about tricks. It's all I know. I don't—' Her voice broke and his hands curled into fists at the hitch in her voice. 'I don't trust what's real. I don't trust myself to see it.'

'Well...' Maybe it was time to bring in light-hearted Max. He sensed she was already telling him more than she was comfortable with. He didn't want the distance to be permanent. After all, they were together for the next forty-eight hours. It might as well be fun.

It went no further than that.

'The joke would be on me if I *was* pulling a sleazy trick. The room between our bedrooms is the size of an average hotel foyer. I think we can both sleep safely tonight.'

'Your virtue was always safe with me,' she said, but she still didn't look at him, and Max noted a flash of red high on her cheekbones.Embarrassment—or something more primal?

The hotel was centrally located, right in the heart of London. Max had travelled to the UK on business many times and was familiar with the hotels, high-end clubs and restaurants of the buzzing city—but he had never wandered aimlessly through the wide city streets, never used the Tube or hopped on a bus. It was freeing. Being part of the city, not observing it through a cab window.

They had wandered south, moving towards the river as if led by a dousing stick, and were now on a wide open street. St James's Park opened out on one side, a city oasis of green and trees in stark contrast to the golden silhouette of Big Ben dominating the skyline in front of them.

'Looks like you got your wish.' Ellie seemed to have recovered her equilibrium. 'We're in tourist central. Shall I buy you a policeman's helmet or a red phone box pencil sharpener?'

'I think I want a Big Ben keychain,' he decided. 'And possibly a shirt that says "You came to London but all you bought me was this lousy T-shirt".'

'As long as you wear it tomorrow night. So what now? We could go into Westminster Abbey? Visit the park? I think I'm allowed in the Houses of Parliament, but I might have needed to arrange it with my MP first.'

'That would be cool. I'd like to watch all your politicians yell at each other. Are you allowed to bring popcorn?'

'Nope, only jellied eels.'

'Only *what*?' She had to be kidding, right?

'They're a London delicacy. All the English love them. We just keep it hidden so the rest of the world doesn't steal our national dish. We usually wash them down with some whelks and a pint of stout.'

'Very funny.'

She laughed. 'It's true. I bet I can find you a place that sells them—if you're man enough to try them.'

'I'll take the slur on my masculinity, thanks.' He shuddered at just the thought of the slimy fish.

'Coward. Right…what would tourists do? The palace is that way.' She pointed to the park. 'And we could take your photo with one of the guards at Horse Guards. That's always popular.'

'If only I was eight… Will we get invited to have tea with the Queen?'

'Now that you've dissed the national dish it's very unlikely. You don't graduate to cucumber sandwiches until you've mastered the jellied eels.'

'Just an unworthy Yank? Another dream shattered.'

Ellie ignored him. 'So, what will it be? Trafalgar Square? Covent Garden? Or we could see a show?'

'You know, I'm pretty much enjoying just walking. Is that okay?'

Surprise flashed across her face. 'Of course.'

Their route continued riverwards to a busy intersection. Cars were such an integral part of all US cities that Max never noticed their noisy intrusion, but they seemed wrong in this ancient city, beeping and revving in front of the old riverside palaces. The road bisected the great houses from the riverfront, with pedestrians crowded onto the grey pavements.

Ellie stopped on the tip of the pavement and directed an enquiring look across the bridge. 'Shall we cross over?'

Max raised an eyebrow. 'To the dark side?'

'It *is* south of the river, but I think we'll be safe.'

'I'll hold you personally responsible for my safety.'

If Max had truly been a tourist, and if he'd had his camera, then he would have stopped halfway across the bridge and, ignoring the mutters of the tourist hordes, photographed the iconic clock tower. But all he had was his phone.

'Come here.' He pulled it out of his pocket and wrapped an arm around Ellie. He felt her stiffen. 'Obligatory Big Ben selfie,' he explained. 'Smile!'

She relaxed, just an iota, but it was enough for her to lean a little further in, for him to notice that there was softness under that slenderness, that her hair smelt of sunshine and the colours were even more diverse close up: coffee and cinnamon, toffee and treacle, shot through with gold and honey.

It took every ounce of self-control he owned not to tighten his arm around her slim shoulders, not to pull her in a little closer, to test just how well they'd fit. Every ounce not to spin her round, not to tilt that pointed chin and claim her mouth. He ached to know how she would taste, to know how she would feel pressed against him.

'Smile!'

Was that his voice? So strained? So unnaturally hearty? But Ellie didn't seem to notice, pulling an exaggerated pout as he pressed the button on the camera.

'One more for luck.' Really he wasn't quite ready to let her go. Not just yet.

CHAPTER SIX

'I'VE GOT IT!'

It was a little exhausting being a tour guide, especially in a city you didn't know that well. Ellie had grown up just thirty miles away from the capital, but her family seldom ventured into the big, bad city.

And when her friends had begun to travel in alone for gigs and shopping, and to find the kind of excitement missing from their little market town, Ellie had been stuck at home, unable to leave her grieving mother.

She still didn't know how her mother had been able just to shut down. To leave her daughter to make every decision, to take responsibility at such a young age for cooking and cleaning and hiding the fact that Ellie was basically raising herself from their neighbours and her teachers.

But Ellie had had no choice. If they had found

out then what would have happened? What if she'd been put into care, the remains of her family shattered?

She had never allowed herself to resent her lonely teen years—at least not until she'd been unceremoniously swept aside when Bill had entered her mother's life. But now, as they wandered towards the South Bank, she couldn't help noticing the gangs of teenage girls dressed to the max, a little too loud, a little too consciously unselfconscious. Young, vibrant, free.

What would she have been if she had ever had the chance to find out who she was? If she hadn't been the dutiful daughter, the besotted young girlfriend too scared to open her mouth for fear of showing her lack of worldliness? And then later the terrified fiancée, softly spoken, anticipatory, as nervous as a doe in hunting season.

But today was her chance. Carefree, no agenda, no expectations—and did it matter if they did get lost?

'Got what?'

'Tourist activity number one.'

Ellie tucked a hand through Max's arm. It

should have been a natural gesture. Friendly. He didn't know that she rarely touched another human being. That the protective cloud she kept swirled around her was physical as well as emotional.

Carefree Ellie wouldn't mind tugging Max down the steps off Westminster Bridge.

Carefree Ellie might be thinking of how it had felt when he'd pulled her in for that selfie. How strong he'd felt. How safe.

Might want him to touch her some more.

Max didn't resist as she pulled him down the steps. It was nice that he made no attempt to take control, to assert himself as the dominant force.

'Okay, don't keep me in suspense.' Max laughed as they came to a stop. 'Where are we headed?'

Ellie put her hands on her hips and shook her head. 'You've got eyes, haven't you? Use them.'

He looked around slowly. London's South Bank was as busy as always, crammed with tourists snapping pictures, kids on skateboards heading towards the famous skate park, people strolling on their way to Tate Modern, to the Globe, to the Royal Festival Hall. Others had stopped to browse at one of the many kiosks selling a myriad of snacks. Behind them a queue snaked out of the open doors of the London Aquarium.

The atmosphere was heated with expectation, with excitement, and yet it was inclusive and friendly, completely different from the fevered, crowded rush of Covent Garden or Oxford Street, more welcoming than the moneyed exclusivity of Knightsbridge.

I could like it here, Ellie realised with a sense of shock. It couldn't be more different from her seaside sanctuary, but there was a warm friendliness and acceptance that pulled at her.

'Um…' Max's eyes were narrowed in thought. 'Are we going to get a boat?'

'No. At least not yet. That might be fun tomorrow, though.'

'Go see some penguins?'

'Oh, I *love* penguins. We should definitely do that. But, no. I gave you a clue when I said to use your eyes.'

Ellie shifted from foot to foot, impatient with his slowness. How could he not see? The dammed thing had to be over one hundred metres high. It wasn't exactly inconspicuous!

She stared at him suspiciously. Was that a smile crinkling the caramel eyes?

'Isn't the Globe along here? Got a hankering for some Shakespeare?'

Every single suggestion sounded perfect, but she shook her head. 'Last guess.'

'Or...? What's the forfeit?' His smile widened. 'There has to be a forfeit or there's no fun...'

Ellie could feel her heart speeding up. A forfeit. Thoughts of kisses sprang unbidden into her mind, thoughts of a winner's claim. Could she suggest it? *Dare* she?

She could see it so clearly... Standing on tiptoe and pulling that dark head down to hers. That moment that felt as if it would last for ever when two mouths hovered, so close and yet not touching, and the *knowing*. The delicious anticipation of knowing that at any second they would meet.

Her stomach dipped. It had been so, *so* long since she had had a first kiss.

'Ellie?'

The teasing note in his voice flustered her, as

if he had read her thoughts. Her cheeks flamed red-hot and she took a step back, all the daring seeping out of her.

'The loser has to buy the winner a souvenir that sums up the day. But it can't cost more than a fiver,' she added. 'That makes it more of a challenge.'

He just looked at her levelly, that same smile lurking in his eyes. 'You never did play dare as a kid, did you, Ellie? Okay, challenge accepted.'

'So? It's not penguins, at least not yet, it's not Shakespeare, and it's not a boat-ride. What's your final answer?'

He grinned wickedly. Damn him, he had been playing her.

'It's a good thing I'm not scared of heights, now...isn't it, honey?'

It soon became obvious that Max Loveday wasn't used to playing the ordinary tourist. Not that surprising, considering his background. From what he had let slip, his holidays were usually spent either in luxurious condos in the Bahamas or in the family home on Cape Cod. His was a life of private jets and town cars, VIP passes and prestige, and Ellie suspected that queueing hadn't played a huge role in his formative years.

It showed. He couldn't keep still, jiggling from foot to foot like an impatient child.

'How long is this going to take?' He craned his neck to look at the queue. 'Why is it so slow?'

'Because each pod only takes a certain amount of people.' Ellie smiled at an excited small girl standing in front of them, holding her mother's hand tightly. 'Be patient.'

'I could have hired out a whole pod just for us. Priority boarding, no standing in line, no sharing. Did you see that you can even have a champagne pod?'

Ellie shook her head at him, although it was hard to keep her mouth from smiling at his wistful tone. 'Yes, but that's not what tourists *do*. Tourists queue. Patiently. Take a selfie of yourself in the queue, and if you're good we'll play I Spy.'

He groaned at the pun and a flutter of happiness lifted her. It was a silly little joke but she had thought of it, shared it. With Simon she had been too busy trying to be informed and appreciative to find the courage to joke around.

She was only twenty-five. It wasn't too late. She looked down the queue: excited families, groups of friends chattering loudly, orderly tour groups patiently waiting. And couples. Everywhere. Arms slung around waists, around shoulders, leaning in, leaning on, whispering, kissing, together.

An ache pulsed in her chest. She had been so glad to get away from Simon, so relieved to be on her own, that the very thought of togetherness had repulsed her. But they had never been 'together' in that way. Not even in the beginning. Simon would never have queued, never have whispered affectionately in her ear, never sneaked a kiss or pulled her in for a longer and very public display of affection.

What must it be like? To be so wrapped up in somebody who was so wrapped up in you? Ellie stole a look at Max. He was leaning against the metal barrier, staring up at the iconic wheel. What would it be like to be wrapped up in Max Loveday?

All those first kisses, all those long walks with no idea about their destination, all those awkward first dates, all those long meals not even noticing the restaurant emptying around them—how many of those simple, necessary, life-affirming things had she been cheated of? How many had she allowed herself to be cheated of?

Maybe she'd licked her wounds in Cornwall long enough.

Ellie didn't say much as they waited—and waited—to board a pod. There was a thoughtful expression on her face that Max was reluctant to disturb, but she perked up when they were finally guided into the slowly moving pod—along with what seemed like hundreds of small uniformed children and two harassed-looking adults.

'I was definitely really bad in a past life,' he whispered to her as the kids crowded in, each of them yelling at what must be several decibels louder than legal limits.

Ellie raised her eyebrows. 'Just in a past life?'

'Believe me, a few student pranks and some

adolescent attitude were not bad enough sins for *this* kind of cruel and unusual punishment.'

'They're having fun, though.' Her lips curved into a smile as she watched the children explore every inch of the pod.

'Yes,' he conceded as he steered her towards a corner. '*Noisy* fun. I vote we stand our ground here.'

'There's plenty of room.' But she put both hands on the window and looked out. 'It's pretty slow, isn't it? I hardly feel like I'm moving.'

'Disappointed? I didn't peg you as a speed queen.'

She just smiled, and they stood in silence for a long moment as the wheel continued its stately turn, lifting them high above the city. The children quietened a merciful amount as their teachers started pointing out places of interest, and filled in the questionnaires they had all been issued with in great concentration.

The pod itself was spacious, its curved glass rising up overhead, providing panoramic three-hundred-and-sixty-degree views.

'I'm glad it's not see-through under our feet.

I'm not sure I want to see the ground falling away.' Ellie shuddered.

'This was *your* idea,' he reminded her as he looked out at the incredible view. 'It's funny, you think of London as an old city, but there's so many skyscrapers. It's completely different to other European capitals, like Paris or Rome. Did you know there's see-through glass on the floor of the Eiffel Tower? Do you think you would be able to stand on that?'

'Possibly…I've never been to Paris, or to Rome.' Her voice was wistful and she continued to stare out at the skyline, her finger tracing it against the glass.

Max opened his mouth to make a flippant promise, but something in her eyes stopped him. If he ever made Ellie Scott a promise he'd need to keep it. And this was one he wasn't sure he could.

A day and a half of fun? An evening of black tie glamour? A joint project? None of them was a heavy or binding commitment. Not together or separately. So why did they feel so important? As if they meant more…as if they could mean everything… There was no way he could or *should* saddle himself with any other responsibilities towards this woman. He'd be back home in a week, and Trengarth nothing but a memory. And that was how it should be.

He had more than enough on his shoulders, thank you very much.

He kept his tone light, teasing, adding much needed distance with his flippancy, 'At the advanced old age of twenty-five you should get booking.'

She didn't respond to the lightness. 'I bet you've been everywhere. Business class and top hotels.'

He grinned at her. 'Totally unlike the hovel we're staying in tonight? DL Media have offices all over the globe. I've been to most.'

She turned then, looked at him with curiosity. 'So you only travel on business? What about for fun? For culture?'

There was a shocked undertone in her voice. It put him on edge, made him feel wanting in some way. As if he'd failed some test. 'I'll have you know there's a lot of culture in your average regional boardroom. And there's nothing as cultural as a red-eye flight and dinner at a five-star restaurant. What?'

She had started to say something and then stopped, as if she'd thought better of it.

She shook her head.

He eyed her narrowly. 'Go on.'

'It's just...' She hesitated again, biting down on her lip, her eyes not meeting his.

'Just...?' he prompted, resisting the urge to fold his arms and stare her down.

'It sounds a little lonely. I mean, you travel all over the world, and I don't really leave Trengarth, but in some ways we're both a little...' She paused, the big dark eyes fluttering up to meet his. 'A little trapped.'

Max couldn't hold back an incredulous laugh. *Trapped?* He was heir to one of the biggest companies in the world. He'd visited most of the major cities in the world. His life was golden—at least it had been.

'Honey, we are *nothing* alike. You choose to hide yourself away in your pretty little seaside village and let your life be lived through the books that you read. *My* life is about responsibilities you'll never understand. Family and employees and a heritage I need to be worthy of.'

She glared at him. 'I understand about family and I understand about responsibility. Scale isn't everything, Max. And if this is the first day you have really allowed yourself to get out of the business district and into the heart of a city then, yes, you are as trapped as I am. You may have set foot in Rome and Paris, but did you *see* them?'

Of course he had seen them! Through glass, mainly. Not like today, obviously, but there wasn't always time, and it wasn't *necessary.* His justifications sounded hollow, even as he thought them.

'The highlights, yes. But I was there to *work*, Ellie.'

'I see.' She turned away and stared out of the window. 'When *I* travel, finally, I want to see it all. Not just the bits the guidebooks show me. I want to walk through the alleyways and eat in the neighbourhood restaurants. I want to find the beating heart of the city and lose myself in it.'

'Then why haven't you?'

It took a while for her to respond, and when she

did her voice was low, as if she were reluctant to admit the truth out loud.

'I was afraid. Afraid I'd be disappointed, afraid I'd get it wrong, afraid it wouldn't live up to my expectations. When you know how it feels to watch your dreams shatter it can be hard to trust in your dreams again.'

'What are your dreams now, Ellie?' His voice lowered as he moved closer to her, the pod all but disappeared, the children forgotten. There was just her and the hopelessness in her voice.

'Once they were the usual, I suppose. University, then a good job, and to fall in love and have children. Lots of children...' Her voice softened. 'I always wished I was part of a big family, and after we lost Dad and Phil I felt even more alone. That's why I loved books, I think. They were the only way I could escape, travel, try new things. I wanted to be Hermione or Lyra or Anne Shirley. Lonely children who forged their own path. Now...? I don't know, Max. I haven't dared dream in such a long time.'

'I've never thought about escape...' He hesitated. That was true, but was it the whole truth?

'I'm under pressure, sure, to be a Loveday is a pretty big responsibility. But it's a privilege too.'

'Do you still feel that way?'

He shook his head slowly. 'You're right. Now I just feel trapped,' he admitted, realising the truth of the words as he said them out loud. 'My dad wants my approval, my mom wants me on-side, and the business needs me to do something clever—soon. It's like everything I grew up thinking I knew was a lie.'

'How so?'

He tried to make sense of his jumbled thoughts. 'We were picture-perfect, you know? Gorgeous house, plenty of money but not showy, members of the right clubs, giving to the right causes…and Grandfather in the centre of it, the benevolent tyrant. I thought he could do no wrong.'

He blew out a breath, some of the weight on his chest lightening as he finally spoke the heretical thoughts aloud.

'But underneath it all Dad was always resentful. I think Grandfather kept him on a tight leash. *And* my mother. In public they were this affectionate couple, but now he's met Mandy I can't help wondering...' His voice trailed off.

'If any of it was real?'

Damn, she was perceptive. 'Oh, he had affairs. I always knew that. All the weekends Dad was working, the extravagant gifts he'd bring back. The hushed rows and then the insistence on putting on a good face in public. But underneath it all I was sure they really loved each other. Now it's all corroded—Mom is so bitter all she can think of is punishing him, no matter that it could bankrupt the company.'

Ellie drew in a deep breath, her eyes searching his face. 'That bad?'

'It's possible,' he admitted. 'And if lawyers get involved it could be a hundred times worse. That's why Dad wants me to negotiate with her. Meanwhile she wants me to promise not to ever engage with Dad's new girlfriend.' He could feel his mouth twist into the kind of cynical smile he'd never worn before this year. 'I guess I've always had to be the sensible one, the adult. I just never resented it before now.'

Her hand fluttered up and for one moment he

thought she was going to touch his face. His chest tightened with anticipation, only for disappointment to flood through his veins as she lowered it again, tucking it behind her with a self-conscious gesture.

He leaned in, one arm on the glass beside her, his eyes fixed on hers. Not touching her, not even invading her space—not really—although the temptation to move that little bit further in was pushing at him…the need to move his hands from the glass to her shoulderblades. To allow them to slide down her narrow back. To feel her shiver under his touch, reining in the urge to rush, making them both wait.

But he couldn't.

Her eyes had widened, her breathing shallow and he didn't know if it was attraction or fear—he'd bet that *she* didn't really know either. There were times when he could swear that she was attracted to him: the way she smiled, ran a hand through her hair, peeped from under her lashes. Even in the line for the London Eye he had caught her looking at him with a speculation that had made his blood heat.

But the next moment she would shut off totally. She was as skittish as an unbroken colt. Part of him needed to know why, wanted to help her, protect her. But he had known her for what...? A few days? Who was he to walk into her life and arrogantly assume he could put it right?

He rocked back on his feet, casually letting his arm fall back, giving her the space she needed. He smiled at her, slow and sweet and as unthreatening as an ice cream sundae.

'Ellie Scott, I do believe we are breaking the rules.'

She was still frozen in place. 'We are?'

'We said we were going to have fun and, believe me, talking about my family is anything but. So, I am going to ask one of those nice teachers for one of their quizzes, and I am going to see if I can beat you and every single one of these ten-year-olds.'

'You don't know what the quiz is actually on.' The colour had come back into her cheeks and her shoulders had relaxed.

'I don't care. Honey, in my family we play to win. Monopoly, Clue, Mario Kart, Singstar—

whatever it is, we do whatever it takes to win. And if that means bribing a ten-year-old for the answers, then watch me go.'

What would have happened if she'd smiled at him instead of standing there like a faun frozen in place by the White Witch? Would he have moved in closer? Would he have touched her? Kissed her?

What must he think? Whether he was just being friendly or was attracted to her he must think her gauche at best, ridiculous at worst.

Not that you would know, because within two minutes he had charmed two quiz sheets out of the bemused teachers and proceeded to barter, beg and bribe answers from the excited group of children, high-fiving them all when they finally exited the pod, the kids to go into the attached museum, Ellie and Max to begin a late-afternoon stroll along the side of the Thames.

'What now? Penguins?' he asked.

She looked at the queue, still snaking around the block, and pulled a face. 'It's a bit late. I don't think we'd get to the front before it shuts. Rain-check?'

'Look.' He stopped beside a poster. 'You can have afternoon tea with them. How cool! Do you think we have to eat raw fish too? I mean, I like sushi as much as the next guy, but I'm not sure I could manage a whole fish, bones and all.'

'Maybe the penguins like scones.' Her eyes flicked over the dates. 'The next one isn't till next month…the twenty-second.'

'Diary it in.' He flashed a grin at her. 'Penguins, sushi, and scones for two.'

'I wouldn't miss it for the world!'

'You still owe me a souvenir,' he reminded her. 'In fact two. I aced that quiz.'

'You cheated at that quiz.'

'The destination is all that matters. How you get there is irrelevant.' He began to stroll along, quite unrepentant.

'Do you really believe that?' Lots of people did, obviously. But she'd expected more of him.

He slid her a sidelong grin. 'Sure I do. Don't worry about who you kick on the way up, 'cause you have no intention of ever coming back down again. Survival of the fittest. Family mottoes, all of them. I bet Great-Aunt Demelza grew up cross-stitching them into samplers so we could hang them on our bedroom walls.'

'Oh, ha-ha.' But she didn't mind the teasing.

A glow spread through her as she watched him from the corner of her eye. Sauntering along, dark hair ever so slightly ruffled, the morning's stubble on his chin. Just another American tourist enjoying the London summer evening.

But not every tourist attracted admiring glances from the groups of girls they passed, and not everyone exuded such happy vibes. Which was a little bizarre, because when they'd first met she hadn't pegged him as the relaxed type. Arrogant? Sure. Rude? Most definitely. It was funny to think that if someone had told her just a few days ago that she would be spending time away with him, that he would make her laugh, make her heart beat faster, she would have laughed—and prescribed a course of wholesome children's books and some early nights.

And yet here she was.

And here *he* was.

She couldn't stop looking at him, fixating on the way the late-afternoon sun glinted on his bare tanned arms, highlighting every play of muscle. How it lingered on his strong, capable hands. Her eyes followed the sun's playful light as it danced over his wrists and along his fingers. What would it be like to hold them? To slide her finger over one knuckle? Could she? Would she dare? All she had to do was reach out.

She swung her hand a little closer in a pathetic experiment, snatching it back in a panic before allowing it to swing again. A jolt shot through her as her knuckles grazed his. It was all she could do not to cling on and never, ever let go.

'Ellie.'

He stopped and turned to face her. There was a simmering heat in his eyes...a heat that mirrored the liquid fire slipping through her veins, setting every nerve alight. Nerves that had spent so long dormant sprang to fiery life.

'If you want to hold my hand, honey, then all you have to do is take it.'

She gaped, trying to formulate some response, to deny it. But she was mute.

'But, Ellie...?'

There was a roughness to his voice, as if he was trying very hard to stay measured, to sound calm. She held his gaze despite the weakness in her knees, the tremors shivering through her. Despite the fear that she was making a mistake, the urge to retreat that was almost as strong as the urge to surge forward.

'Yes?'

'If you do then I *will* kiss you. Maybe not here, in front of all these people, and maybe not as we walk, but some time, at some point, I will kiss you. And you…' his eyes dropped to her mouth in an almost physical caress '…you'll kiss me back. Are you ready for that, Ellie?'

It wasn't the heat. Not in the end. And it wasn't the rough edge to his voice that spoke of want and passion. It wasn't his words and the arrogant assumption implicit in them. It was the tone. It was the look in his eyes. A look that said he needed her. That if she turned away he would accept it—and regret it.

And she? Would she regret it too? Just as she was beginning to regret the years she had spent hidden away, as safe as a nun in her convent and as chaste—not through vocation but through fear.

Ellie lifted her chin. She was done hiding and she was done living her life in the shadows. She was going to live. She was going to risk.

Slowly, hating the giveaway trembling of her fingers, she extended her arm and slipped her hand into his. His fingers closed around her, one at a time, softly, as if he knew not to spook her. His hand was warm, comforting, strong—and just the sense of skin against skin sent sparks dancing throughout her body. A line connected her fingertips to the pit of her stomach.

'Shall we?'

Max took a step forward and Ellie watched her arm move with him, feeling the tug on her body to fall into step behind him. And as if in a dream she followed, her stride matching his, their bodies working together. Fitting together.

She didn't know where they were headed, and right now she didn't much care. As long as her hand was in his they could walk for ever while she remembered what it felt like to yearn, to want to touch.

It felt good.

CHAPTER SEVEN

HE STILL HADN'T kissed her.

What kind of man promised a girl that he would kiss her and didn't deliver? He hadn't even come tantalisingly close. Not so much as an intimate smile all evening.

Not in their stroll along the South Bank, even though their hands had been entwined the whole time. Not as they'd perused the secondhand book stalls, nor as they'd bought milkshakes from one of the many vendors. Not over a glass of wine in a quaintly half-timbered pub, nor over dinner in a tiny Italian restaurant where the pasta had tasted the way Ellie had always imagined real Italian food would.

She'd closed her eyes and listened to the shouting from the kitchen, breathed in the mingled smells of tomato, basil and wine, and had almost imagined that she was in Rome at last.

And now they were returning to the hotel, retracing their steps along the riverside path, lit up and vibrant with the evening crowd. They were holding hands once again and he still hadn't made one single move towards her.

If she burst with anticipation it would be more than a little messy—and it would totally serve him right.

He shouldn't make promises he wasn't prepared to follow through.

'Are you tired? We could get a cab? Or,' he added a little doubtfully, 'as we're being tourists we could try buses. But I have to warn you they confuse the hell out of me.'

'Do they really confuse you or have you just never been on one?'

She was pretty sure it was the latter. He might be dressed down, but he was designer all the way at heart. She simply couldn't imagine him on a bus.

He grinned. 'Both.'

'I'm fine walking. I ate so much pasta I could do with the exercise.' *Very, very cool, Ellie.* That was definitely not in the 'Things to Say on a First Date' guide.

Not that this was. A first *or* a date. Obviously.

'I don't know what you're thinking, but I can tell there's a lot of wheels turning in that head of yours. Anything you want to share?'

How could he sound so relaxed? So amused?

Because this wasn't a first date. Holding hands with someone you'd known for a less than a week and only occasionally liked was probably completely normal to him.

'No.' She wasn't lying. She didn't want to share a single thought about dates or kisses with him. 'I'm not really thinking about anything. Just that it's nice to be out and about.'

'What shall we do tomorrow? The car is coming to pick us up at six and you'll probably need a good hour and a half to get ready…'

Ellie was about to interrupt. To tell him she only needed half an hour. A quick shower, brush her hair, slick on some mascara and lipstick and decide between her not that little black dress or her slightly longer black dress, put on her black almost-heels. It was hardly the routine of a diva.

Although she *could* visit the hotel spa and get her nails done. It would probably wipe out her entire savings, but a little bit of pampering would be nice.

Ellie watched a group of girls totter past, only just balancing on their high strappy shoes. They were like a flock of exotic birds as they trilled and giggled in tiny, sheer summer dresses in emerald and cobalt blue, silver and sunshine-yellow.

Young, vibrant and alive.

She looked down. Skinny grey jeans. Again. High-top trainers. Again. Another short-sleeved tunic, black this time. Her hair was still twisted in the loose knot she had put it into that morning; her face was make-up free. The brightest colour in her wardrobe was a deep purple. She had switched the taupes and beiges that Simon had approved of for another colourless uniform. Another way to blend in.

The knowledge that she had chosen her own uniform didn't make it feel any better. Or any less constraining.

'Actually…' She spoke quickly before she changed her mind. 'I'll need longer than that. I might need the whole afternoon.'

Max's mouth quirked. 'Of course. *Just* the whole afternoon?'

Guilt pulled at her. 'I know we were supposed to be having fun. I'll be around in the morning to do something.'

'No, it's fine.' He pulled a face. 'I always planned to be in the office tomorrow anyway. I can't really play hooky on a Monday, and there's still so much to do in Trengarth even if I employ someone to empty the house, I might not get back to London this trip. Take as long as you need.'

He didn't tell her that she didn't need the afternoon, didn't waste time on fake compliments or try and talk her out of it. He respected her decision. That was great.

Or, more honestly, it was a little disappointing. But that was okay. She'd prove to Max Loveday that she could scrub up as well as any of his high-maintenance, trust fund, well-bred, moneyed usual dates.

And she'd prove to herself that it wasn't too late to take a chance.

* * *

He still hadn't kissed her. He knew that she wanted him to. Hell, she'd given him her hand, hadn't she? Had stared at him with those Bambi eyes and slipped those slender fingers through his, trembling as if she were abseiling over a cliff and he was her lifeline. It was a little terrifying.

It was intoxicating.

And he wanted to kiss her.

Wanted to so much he was almost trembling with it too. *Almost.*

And that was partly why he was holding back. This was a short trip and anything—anyone—he got entangled with had to be on a strictly short-term basis. Right now, what with all the crazy in his life, that was fine by him.

Besides, this was exactly what he didn't need long-term. This kind of messy emotion. Sure it felt right *now*, but what about next week? Next year? With an ocean between them and completely separate lives? It would be insanity.

Once he'd kissed Ellie would he remember that? Or would he be drawn in too far? Into something he didn't have the time or the head space to handle?

That was only partly it, though. Because it was all very well thinking about the future, but when all was said and done it would only be one kiss. But over the last two hours he'd sensed that it would be so much more to Ellie. Skittish, wide-eyed, and more vulnerable than she knew. It would be so easy to hurt her without even trying, and he didn't want to be that guy.

He shouldn't have offered…should have known better. But the words were said now. He couldn't take them back.

And honestly…? He wasn't sure he would if he could.

But he hadn't kissed her. Not yet.

Their walk was over in the blink of an eye. He must have found his way back to the hotel by luck rather than judgement, because all he'd been aware of was the feel of her hand in his. The knowledge that at any second he could pull her closer and she wouldn't stop him.

How could he not?

How *could* he?

Suddenly the shared suite didn't seem quite so funny, and the sitting-room separating their rooms seemed far too small. He wanted locks, corridors, possibly a couple of floors between them.

The hotel lobby was brightly lit, with the crystals in the chandeliers dancing rainbows, casting light onto the ornate gilt walls. Ellie seemed to have shaken off her earlier nervousness and walked confidently over to the reception desk, where a perfectly groomed woman sat. Heads together, voices low, they shared a long conversation before Ellie swivelled and walked back over to him.

'All set.' She had a mysterious expression on her face, like a child on Christmas Eve, ripe with secrets. 'Ready?'

'Absolutely.' *Not.*

Her didn't take her hand, stayed a safe distance away as they took the lift up to their floor, as they walked the few short metres to their suite. He stood gallantly back, allowing her into the sitting-room before him. But his promise was hanging in the air between them. It was in every questioning glance, every rise of her chest, every nervous flutter of her hands.

'Nightcap?' He shouldn't have made the suggestion, should simply say goodnight and get out of there. But his common sense had been overridden by his need to extend the evening even by just a few minutes.

Ellie was standing in the middle of the sitting-room, her slim, casually clad figure incongruous amongst the deep purples and gold luxury of the opulent suite. She looked as fresh as a wildflower set amidst hothouse blooms.

'No, thank you.' She turned slowly. 'I don't think I fully took this in earlier. It's very…'

'Gold?' he offered.

Her mouth tilted. 'It is that. It's all very imposing, isn't it? I'm not sure it's exactly homely, though. I can't imagine myself sprawling out on that sofa, for instance.'

Max took a deep breath. Ellie. *Sprawled. Sofa.*

His mind was full of images. Tousled hair, swollen lips, languid eyes, creamy skin…

'I would like to see that.' His voice was low, a rough rasp.

Time stopped. Her eyes flickered to his and stayed there. Neither of them able to look away as his words reverberated around the room.

It was no use. What was it they said about good intentions? And if his feet were already set on the path to hell then he might as well enjoy the journey.

'Max?'

He didn't know if she had said his name or just mouthed it, but it was too late. He was past the point of thought. Of common sense.

It took him just two strides to stand before her.

The blood was rushing through his veins, boiling hot, and his pulse was beating louder, harder than it had ever beat before. There was a deep ache in his chest that could only be assuaged by one thing. By her.

He stepped closer and waited, a bare millimetre between them. He needed her to make the final move, to show that she was in on this. Whatever 'this' was. Whatever 'in' meant.

'Ellie?' Not a command, not even a question. More a query.

Her eyes were huge, dark, desire mingling with

doubt. He could overcome that doubt, kiss it out of her. But he waited. Waited for her to come to him. This had to be her decision.

His hands tingled, desperate to touch her, but he kept them at his sides.

She swallowed, a convulsive movement. Then she stepped forward.

They stood there for one second. It was an eternity. He could feel the full softness of her breasts against his chest, her legs just brushing his, her hands soft on his shoulders. Her face was tilted up towards his.

Max didn't know who made the next move. Whether or not she stood on tiptoe just as he bent forward. But their lips met, found each other as if of their own volition. And he was lost.

Lost in her scent, in her taste. Lost in the grip of her hands on his shoulders. Lost in the curve of her waist, the slenderness of her back as his arms encircled her to pull her closer.

He hadn't meant this. He had meant a soft kiss, a teasing kiss, a flirtatious kiss. But this…? This was hot and greedy and needy and all-encompassing.

He pulled her in closer, crushing her body against his, needing to feel her moulded to him. And she pressed closer yet, wrapped herself round him as if a millimetre gap was too much. And it was.

His hands moved up her back, learning her curves as they went, until finally they were buried in the glorious weight of her silky hair. It was everything he had hoped for: fine, soft, wound around his hands.

All promises of not going too fast disappeared. He needed to see her clad in nothing but that hair…needed to explore every inch of her, touch every inch. And Ellie was with him every step, her soft hands burning a trail as they slid beneath his T-shirt, roaming across his back, across his chest, and then slowly, tantalisingly, but so very surely, moving lower, across his abdomen, and then lower still.

Max sucked in a deep breath as she reached his belt. Her hands were trembling but sure as she unbuckled his belt, moving her fingers to the first button on his jeans.

He caught her busy hands in his. 'Slow down, honey. We have all night.'

He allowed his voice to linger suggestively on the last two words and heard her gasp as his hands slid over hers, then moved slowly, oh, so slowly, his fingers caressing the soft skin of her wrists, her delicate inner elbow and up to her shoulders. He held her loosely for one moment, his lips travelling down, across her pointed chin, down her neck to feast briefly on her throat.

She was utterly still, her head thrown back to allow him access, the only sign of life her rapidly beating pulse, its overheated beat marching in step with the rapid thump of his heart. And then he moved, scooping her up in his arms, his mouth back on hers, needing, demanding, wanting as he carried her across the room and through the door. Her arms were wrapped around his neck, holding on tight, holding *him* tight.

There was no letting go. There was no going back. There was only this. Darkness, touch, moans and need. Only them. Clothes were pulled off with no care for little things like buttons. Impatient, greedy hands pushed barriers aside. Until there were no barriers left…

She should have been thinking, *What have I done?*

Instead all she could think was, *Can we do that again?*

Ellie had never had a morning after the night before. She had never done a walk of shame in last night's dress, with smeared make-up, shoes in hand, tiptoeing out through the door in the grey dawn light. Never woken up next to someone alive with the possibility of a new beginning.

She'd dated Simon for several months before they'd first slept together, and by then she'd been so besotted and so terrified of disappointing him that she had been unable to think or dream about anything but him. Her first thought on waking then hadn't been excitement or happiness but worry—the familiar gnaw of panic. Had she passed muster? Had her youth and inexperience been too obvious? Had she disgusted him?

She couldn't remember enjoying it. It had all been about *him*.

Now she could see that was exactly what Simon had wanted. Could see how he had fed on her toxic mixture of inexperience, loneliness and need. Had encouraged it until she had been exactly what he'd wanted her to be: compliant, dependent and afraid.

So waking up alone, sated, in a strange bed, naked and with every muscle aching in a curiously pleasant way was far too much of a novelty for a previously engaged woman of twenty-five. But there it was.

Alone. Ellie wasn't sure whether relief or indignation was at the forefront of her mind when she rolled over to pat nothing but cold sheets.

Relief that she didn't have to worry about her hair, her breath, the etiquette—should she go in for a kiss or sit up primly and pretend that she *hadn't* nibbled her way over his entire body in lieu of dessert?

Or indignation that she was waking up alone with just a note to remind her that she hadn't dreamt the previous night? *A note!*

There it was on the bedside table, crisp and white like in a scene from a film.

Dear Ellie

You looked so peaceful I didn't like to wake you. I should never have agreed to go in to the office—they called a meeting for nine a.m.

Hope your day is a lot more fun than mine. I'll pick you up at six. Enjoy.

Max

PS Room Service is on DL Media, so go wild. One of us should.

Hmm… She read it through again. It wasn't a love letter—there were no declarations of undying devotion—but neither was it a 'Dear John'. It was something in between.

Which was about right, she supposed.

Ellie rolled over and stretched, enjoying the sheer space of the enormous bed. She could lie lengthways, diagonally, horizontally and still sprawl out in comfort. In fact, now she was thinking about it, she had covered pretty much every inch of the bed last night.

Heat returned to her cheeks as images flashed through her mind, her nerves tingling in sensory recognition. She sat up and looked at the rumpled pillows, the dishevelled sheets. At the clothing still distributed across the room. Her jeans, her tunic. Oh, goodness! Was that her comfortable yet eminently sensible bra?

She covered her face with her hands. Her first ever night of red-hot seduction and she had been wearing underwear as alluring as a nice cup of tea and a custard cream.

At least she hadn't been wearing it for too long. And Max hadn't seemed to have had any complaints. Not judging by the intake of breath when he'd pulled her tunic over her head, and not judging by the heat in his eyes when he had looked at her as if she were the most desirable thing he had ever seen.

Had that been *her*? Prim Ellie Scott? So wanton, so demanding, so knowing? And now that she had allowed that side of her to surface could she lock herself away again? Slide back into her hermit ways and keep this side of herself hidden?

The thing was, she didn't want to explore it with just anyone.

Ellie slumped back onto the bed, the twist of desire in her stomach knotting into dread.

'It's a crush,' she said aloud, emphasising every word slowly and clearly. 'You can't fall in love with someone after a week. Not because they quite fancy you and make you laugh. You are *not* going to become besotted with someone you barely know. Not again.'

It was as if cold water had been thrown over her. All the fire, all the sparks at her nerve-endings extinguished by reality. Ellie shivered, pulling the quilt back over her body, wanting to be warm, to be comforted. To be hidden away.

I won't let the memory of Simon spoil this, she told herself fiercely, blinking hard, refusing to let the threatening tears fall. *I am older, I am most definitely wiser, and I am not the naïve little girl I was back then. I know what this is and I can handle it. He'll be flying back home in just over a week. Enjoy it.*

She pulled the quilt tighter still, letting its warmth permeate her goosebumped body. This was supposed to be fun, not a trip down Memories I Would Much Rather Forget Lane.

She had plans today. Big, scary and long overdue plans. What was she going to do? Hide in this bed until six or get up, get dressed and follow through? She had allowed Simon to control the last three years of her life just as much as he had controlled the three years they had spent together. She might have plucked up the courage to leave and start afresh, but she hadn't moved on…not really.

And now Max. Offering her the opportunity to explore a new side of herself. A more adventurous side. To be the Ellie she'd always intended to be before her life had been so brutally derailed.

She could take the opportunity he was offering—or she could pack up and go home. Hide away with her books for the rest of her life.

Ellie sat up again and pushed the quilt away. She was going to get up, she was going to order the most decadent breakfast on the room service menu, and she was going to follow every single part of her tentative plan.

And today was the very last day she was going to allow Simon to cast a shadow over her life. He wasn't going to taint a single second of her future. She was finally going to be free.

Meetings, meetings, meetings... Normally Max's head would be spinning with the day he had spent. The London office was the most important after their New York headquarters, and on Max's last visit eighteen months ago it had been a vibrant place full of enthusiasm and talent. Now it was full of fear, with people clinging on to their jobs determinedly or leaving, like rats jumping from a ship before they were pushed.

His father hadn't even been over, having sent in management consultants instead to shake things up. They had certainly managed that—the MD Max had worked so successfully with was long gone and in his place a board full of yes-men with no ideas of their own.

It had put the present state of DL Media into stark perspective. Max might have no appetite for a family rift, but he didn't have much choice. There was far too much at stake: jobs, the company's reputation. His grandfather's legacy.

It should be weighing on his mind, his mood

should be murkier than a classic London pea-souper, and yet all he had wanted all day was to stride out of that infernal boardroom, find Ellie and take her right back to bed. And stay there. The awards ceremony be damned.

He curled his hands into loose fists and took in a deep, shuddering breath. He could have made his excuses and gone. But he had stayed. Because when the chips were down he was a Loveday. Old school. Bred in his grandfather's image. So he had stayed, listened, learned and reassured.

He had ordered his dinner suit to be brought to the building, the car to pick him up straight from there. Had put the business first and his own desires second.

Like a Loveday should.

But it all felt so hollow. No thrill of business. Just the sense of another day wasted. Thank goodness for tonight.

Only Ellie wasn't waiting in the foyer. The car had pulled up outside the hotel and for ten minutes Max waited, his phone in his hand, sending email after email to his long-suffering PA. She had been expecting a quiet week or two. Well, this was going to put paid to any plans she might have had of stepping up her flirtation with Eduardo in Accounts.

Another minute, another email.

Max checked the time. Ellie was fifteen minutes late.

Had she got his note? Had he not been clear? Had she taken offence and hightailed it back to Cornwall? He'd meant to call. He *should* have called.

But for once in his glib life he had been unsure what to say. *Thank you*? *That was incredible*? *All I can think about is touching you*?

He bit back a laugh. Absolutely pathetic. But he still couldn't think of anything better.

He checked his watch again, aware of the chauffeur's eyes on him, the engine idling. He could call.

Or he could go and get her. A gentleman always did. What would his grandfather say if he could see him sitting in a car waiting for her to come to him? He would be horrified.

It only took him a couple of minutes to walk up to their suite, but Max's heart was hammering as if he had climbed to the top of a skyscraper. He was convinced that he would open the door and be confronted by an empty suite. That he had blown it.

He had never worried before. Never waited, never chased. The second it got demanding or difficult he was out of there. He knew all too well where tears, tantrums and demands led. Had grown up with their devastation.

The door handle was slippery in his hand, reluctant to turn, but finally he had swung the door open and he strode into the opulent sitting-room.

'Ellie?'

'I'm in here.' There was nervousness to her voice, a hint of panic. 'Sorry… It all took a little longer than I thought. High-maintenance really is a full-time job. Are we late?'

Max didn't know just how deep a breath he was holding until he heard her voice. The relief hit him with an almost physical force.

'No, my grandfather told me to always pick a time half an hour in advance. It's never steered me wrong yet.'

'Then I've been panicking for nothing?' Her

voice had switched from nervous to indignant. 'Honestly, Max, that was mean.'

He was going to reply. He was. But then she appeared at the door and he couldn't say anything at all. All he could do was stare. He was aware in some dim corner of his mind that his mouth was hanging open, and with some effort he snapped it shut.

And then he stared some more.

Gone was the elusively pretty girl. Here instead was a stunningly beautiful woman.

'Ellie? Wow. You look…' It wasn't the smoothest line, but it was all he could manage. Then, 'You cut your hair.'

That shimmering mass was gone. In its place was an edgy bob, cut in sharp layers. It framed her face, emphasising her eyes, her chin, her defined cheekbones.

'Yes.' Her hand reached up to touch the ends, tentative, as if she couldn't quite believe it. 'I thought it was time.'

'You look incredible.' His voice was hoarse and he couldn't stop staring.

From the tips of her newly styled hair and her

heavily kohled eyes to the scarlet dress, bare at her shoulders, tight-fitting down her torso, then flaring out to mid-thigh, this was a new, dangerous, deeply desirable Ellie.

'Is it too much?' The expectant expression on her face had been replaced with panic. 'Am I overdressed? Have I gone a bit over the top? I can change.'

Yes. She was. Simultaneously over and underdressed. Overdressed because he wanted to tear that dress off her right now. And underdressed because he wasn't sure he wanted his colleagues to see quite so much of her creamy skin. He knew just what long, perfect legs she had. He just didn't want anyone else to appreciate them. Maybe she had a shawl? And some leggings?

He shook his head. What was happening to him? He was thinking like a Neanderthal. His last ex had spent most of the spring in tightfitting yoga pants and a crop top and he had never once cared.

'Max?'

He held out his hand. 'No, don't change a thing. You are absolutely perfect.'

CHAPTER EIGHT

ELLIE HAD ALWAYS thought that she hated small talk.

Standing at Simon's side, her role had been to agree with him. It had been the easiest and the safest thing to do. He wouldn't retreat into one of his terrifying sulks if she didn't say anything wrong.

Of course she couldn't be too mute—then he would accuse of her being dull, of not trying hard enough. No, it had been easier to agree with him at all times.

Tonight was as different from a night out with Simon as a glass of vintage champagne was from cheap lemonade.

Max had made no attempt to keep her near him. But his eyes sought her out as she moved from group to group, catching her gaze with an intimate smile that heated her through. And he'd made sure she was introduced to his companions, supplied with a drink. If she found herself alone even for a second then he was there, as if by magic, ready to introduce her to another key contact.

He would whisk her away, off into a corner, every now and then. She usually had to slip into the cloakroom afterwards and reapply her lipstick. Every time she did she would stop and look at the girl in the mirror. The girl with the emphasised eyes, the choppy hair. The girl in the red dress.

She couldn't hide. Not like this. Her dress was so bright, the cut exposing far more of her arms and legs than she ever usually showed, her hair left her face and her shoulders bare, and her make-up was dramatic.

She was so used to hiding behind her hair she felt exposed without it. But she also felt free, reinvented. It had been long for so many years: one length for her ballet dancing youth, uncut in her teens because her father had loved it so, and her mother would have been devastated if it was cut.

And Simon had liked long hair on women.

She had thought about changing it, in the three years she had spent in Trengarth, but had clung on to the security blanket it offered.

There was no blanket now.

This girl had to mingle, to talk.

And people wanted to talk to *her*, to know her, to discuss her shop, the tentative festival plans. They were interested in her thoughts, in her perspective.

It was a heady experience. For so long she had listened to the voices in her head telling her she was too young, too inexperienced, that she was hampered by her lack of a degree, unable to follow her dreams—and yet at some point in the last three years she had accumulated huge amounts of industry knowledge.

She was on the front line. She knew what people wanted to read, how they wanted to purchase it, what made them angry, excited—and what left them cold. Her best book club meetings were always those where the participants were polarised. And here she was, surrounded by people who spoke her language, people who knew the prefix to most ISBN numbers, got excited by new covers and new releases. People who openly admitted to sniffing the crisp new pages of a paperback book. She was in her element.

And Max allowed her the freedom to fly.

He didn't look as if he were having quite so good a time. Oh, sure, to the casual observer he probably looked as if he was enjoying himself, standing in a group, his stance relaxed, a smile on his face. But there was a tension in his shoulders, a crinkle around his eyes that gave Ellie an inkling that he was hiding his true feelings.

Not surprisingly, here in a room full of industry professionals, rumours about DL Media were running rife. And there was no escape for him in the endlessly moving, speculating, keen-eyed crowd. He wouldn't even be able to relax over dinner. There were no formal tables nor a sit-down meal. Instead endless trays of canapés circulated. It was like dinner in miniature: teeny tarts, quiches, curls of lettuce hiding a quail's egg in their leaves, delicate slivers of cheese and quince.

Normally the very word 'circulate' would bring Ellie out in a cold sweat, but tonight she was managing it effortlessly...despite the pinch of her new and alarmingly high shoes. She had a glass of wine in one hand, something delicious swiped off a passing tray in the other, and interesting conversation.

It beat The Three Herrings pub quiz. Well, apart from the night she had helped win it. That had been pretty spectacular.

'So, DL Media are sponsoring your festival?'

Ellie had to pinch herself as she remembered that she was talking to an agent: a real, live literary agent whose clients included several of her favourite authors.

He tilted his head to one side, his eyes sharp. 'Does that mean you'll only be working with their writers?'

'No!' It wasn't the first time she had heard this. News obviously spread through the publishing world at the same speed with which it rushed through Trengarth—and with the same accuracy. 'The sponsorship comes from Demelza Loveday's personal estate. Max is festival director, but as a family member, not a representative of DL Media.'

'A good thing, if half the rumours I've heard are true.' The agent's eyes were still fastened on her questioningly. 'Is it true their book publishing division is being sold off?'

'I heard they were going digital only.' Another person had joined the group, her face avid with the desire for information.

'Either way, I would be *very* concerned about placing a client with them,' said the agent.

'All rumours of DL Media's demise are very much exaggerated.'

Max's drawl broke into the conversation, much to Ellie's relief.

'It is possible to be both cutting edge *and* traditional, you know. Ellie, I believe the awards are about to start, and they want nominees to be near the front. Just in case your name gets called. Excuse us, please…duty calls. Here's my card. Call me. I am more than happy to continue this conversation with you later.'

His voice was calm, with that slightly arrogant edge, but the hand that held Ellie's arm was gripping tightly.

'Vultures,' he muttered.

'They're just trying to pry.'

'They're not *trying*. They're doing a fine job.' He shook his head. 'Just a hint of this kind of instability and the whole company could crumble faster than a sandcastle at low tide. You heard Tom Edgar then. If he isn't going to consider our bids then we could lose out on new authors, or on re-signing profitable ones. He has a lot of clout.'

'So what are you going to do?'

'Right now? Smile, deny, and make sure you have a great evening. Tomorrow…? Tomorrow I make some serious plans. Right, no more looking so downcast. This isn't my night. It's yours. We need to be ready to toast your success as Independent Bookseller of the Year.'

She laughed, the embarrassed heat flooding her cheeks. 'Shush, this is England. We don't boast. We shuffle in a self-deprecating way and mutter that every other competitor is far more deserving and we didn't expect to win anyway.'

'Ah, but you're with an ignorant Yank, and *we* shout our successes loud and proud.'

'I haven't actually won,' she pointed out.

'Yet.' He was looking more relaxed, the lines

of strain around his mouth evening out. 'I for one am ready to cheer very loudly indeed.'

'Shh!' But she was smiling. 'It's about to start.'

It was a very long ceremony. It seemed as if there was no aspect of the book trade, from industry blogs to conferences, supply chains to sales reps, that wasn't being honoured. Ellie shifted from aching foot to aching foot, wishing she had actually tried walking in her shoes before buying them.

'You're on.'

Max's breath skimmed over her ear as he whispered, the warmth penetrating her skin, and the desire to lean back warred with the nerves jumping in her stomach like a basket of naughty kittens.

'I wish we hadn't come,' she murmured, and he chuckled, low and deep, a hand at her back. To reassure her or to keep her there? Not that she could run away in these shoes…

Best Chain Bookstore, Best Bookshop Manager, Best Event Organiser… On and on the awards went, and the pain in her feet competed with the increasing nausea gnawing away at her.

'Ellie Scott!'

The sound of her name echoed around the room as applause and a couple of cheers greeted it. She stood rooted to the spot in disbelief and embarrassment as, true to his word, Max whooped.

'Me?'

'Go on.' He gave her a gentle push. 'They're waiting for you.'

Ellie hadn't lied when she'd said she didn't expect to win—she worked alone, in a small shop miles away from the capital. Who *knew* her? Of course a quirky city independent would win, she hadn't even bothered to prepare a speech.

The sound of Max's continuing whoops rang in her ears as she stumbled in her unaccustomed heels to the podium. The glare of the lights, the people—so many people—all staring at her, smiling at her. Waiting for her.

Waiting for her to speak.

She was alone under the spotlight of their gaze. Once, long ago, she had enjoyed drama lessons, even taken part in school plays. Now she could barely recognise that girl who had soaked up the audience's attention, but there must be some residual atom of her left, because her shoulders straightened, her voice strengthened.

'When I opened a bookshop people said I was crazy…' A ripple of amusement passed through the crowd and, emboldened by their response, she carried on. 'They thought I should open a coffee shop and have a few books dotted around. Well, I do have a temperamental coffee machine. But it's not the main attraction. The books are.'

She paused, trying to formulate her thoughts.

'It's not easy, and if I had a pound for every time someone has told me the book trade is dead my cash flow would be incredible. I can't compete with the internet giants. I can't stop people browsing and buying the eBook later. But I can—I can and I *do*—offer a tailored service. I can make book-buying fun, informative and easy. I can *recommend*. Of course I have to diversify, and not just with coffee. I run book groups for all ages, knitting groups, craft groups. I go into local schools and playgroups and to WI meetings. I open seven days a week and I stay open late.'

She looked out over the anonymous sea of people and swallowed, panic beginning to twist her chest. Who was *she* to think that she could tell one single person in this room how to sell books? Who did she think she was?

She was twenty-five, and she had run her own business for three years. She wasn't rich, but the shop was in the black and they had chosen *her* to win this award. That was who she was.

'Next year I'll diversify even further, when I curate the first Trengarth Literary Festival. But at the heart of all this diversification is one very simple mission. To get the great stories around out there, into people's hands. That's what they want. Great stories. You keep producing them and I'll keep selling them. Thank you.'

'That was pretty amazing.' Max sat back in the taxi. Amazing for Ellie, a battle for him. But he wasn't going to ruin her triumph by telling her so.

'I know!'

Ellie was glowing, the streetlamps spotlighting her in gold as the car drove them through the well-lit streets. Her hair shone, her dress glittered, but the most luminous thing of all was her smile, stretched wide across her face.

‘I spoke to so many lovely people and they were so kind. Loads of them want to be part of the literary festival. I have so many business cards I don’t know where to start. I thought the first year would be a really small affair, but it really looks like we might attract some big names.’

‘And thanks to Great-Aunt Demelza you can actually *pay* your participants,’ he reminded her. ‘From what I hear that’s by no means usual… especially for start-up festivals. Many of them rely on goodwill alone. A pay cheque will definitely pull people in. But I wasn’t talking about the festival. I was talking about *you*. About your speech.’

‘Oh…’ She flushed, her cheeks coming close to matching the vibrant colour of her dress. ‘That wasn’t a speech. It was…’

‘A call to arms?’

‘No! A few panicked words, that’s all.’

He inched a little closer on the seat so their legs were touching, his knee firmly pressed against hers like a high school boy on a first date, sharing a booth. ‘You inspired me.’

‘Really?’

'Oh, yes. In fact you have been inspiring me all evening.'

'Inspiring you to concentrate on the books side of the business?'

He slid his hand up her leg. Her stockings were a flimsy barrier. How much further was the hotel?

'Amongst other things.'

Her eyebrows rose as she leaned a little closer, her body heating him wherever they touched.

'We *do* have a day of missed fun to make up for. You spent it in meetings and, although some women might find spas and boutiques relaxing, I was terrified the whole time. We could both do with some relaxing.'

'Is that so? And did you have anything in particular in mind?'

Ellie put her hand over his, the pressure moulding his fingers around her leg. 'I'm sure we can work together to think of something.'

Her hand was warm, her fingers wound through his. Was this really the same girl who had jumped like a skittish kitten whenever he touched her? Had the dress and radical haircut given her a new confidence? Or had she been there all the time? Hidden behind the layers and the no-nonsense demeanour?

If only there was more time to explore her, to explore *them*.

'It's our last night in London. We should make it memorable.'

It did no harm to remind her—to remind himself—that this trip was finite. That although he would be returning to Cornwall with her in the morning his holiday was nearly at an end.

'Real life again tomorrow.' She sounded wistful. 'I didn't even want to come here and I've had such an amazing time. I'm not quite ready for it to end—and we didn't get to see the penguins.'

Was she talking about not wanting the trip to end—or not wanting to stop spending time with Max himself? His hand stilled under hers.

'The penguins aren't going anywhere. We could see them in the morning.'

'No, I need a reason to make sure I come back. Besides, now I know I can have scones with them I won't settle for anything less.'

'Of course you'll come back. *We'll* come back.'

We? Where had *that* come from? Max didn't usually like to make plans too far in advance. Previous relationships had begun to fracture when he had refused to commit to a wedding or a family party several months in advance.

Here he was making promises for an unspecified future date.

And it didn't make him want to run.

It was because they had barely begun. He might not be the king of long-term relationships, but neither was he a one-night stand kind of guy. He liked a relationship to run its course.

That was why he was feeling odd about knowing he would have to leave in the next few days. She would be unfinished business, that was all.

'Max?'

She was sitting there, her hand still in his, as lost in her own thoughts as he was in his.

'Yeah?'

'Thank you.'

'Honey, you don't have to thank me for anything.'

'No, I *do*.' She paused, pulling her hand away from his and shifting in her seat so that she was looking directly at him. 'I didn't want to admit it, especially not to myself, but I *was* hiding in Trengarth. I'm twenty-five and the highlight of my week is the pub quiz at The Three Herrings. And I only turn up to that once every few months.'

His body tensed. 'Why were you hiding?'

She didn't answer for a moment, her hands twisting in her lap. 'I didn't trust myself.' Her voice was low, as if she were in the confessional. 'I made a couple of bad choices. I think it made me afraid to try again. After Dad and Phil died Mum clung to me. I let that be my excuse for putting off university, for not starting my own life. But I think I was just too scared. Losing them was like losing a part of myself, losing my identity, and I just couldn't pick myself up again.'

He couldn't imagine it…having your life ripped apart before it had fully begun. 'You were very young.'

Her mouth turned up in a sad approximation of a smile. 'I suppose. But at home I had to be the adult and I allowed it. I allowed Mum to rely on me…allowed her neediness to define me. So when she met Bill and didn't need me any more it was like...like...'

'Like you'd lost everything?'

'Yes. It was exactly like that. And then there was Simon. I was so vulnerable, so lonely when I met him. I guess he sensed that. I thought he was my knight in shining armour. He was ten years older than me and so sure of himself. I was blinded by him, by what he wanted from me I didn't have to figure myself out.'

She had barely mentioned her past, and her fiancé had been no more than a name, but Max's jaw clenched at the sorrow and hurt in her voice. It hadn't been just a relationship gone wrong. She had been badly wounded and her scars evidently still ran deep.

His hands curled into fists. How could anyone hurt her? Strip away her confidence?

'I was so proud of myself for getting away. I thought it was enough...thought that I was finally living the life I wanted. I live in a place I love, doing something I feel passionately about. And those are *good* choices. They *do* make me happy. But as a human being I am still a complete mess.

I don't have many friends, and I don't leave my comfort zone. Not ever. I didn't dare dream of anything else, anything more. Especially not romance. Especially not love.'

Her voice broke a little on the last word.

Max was frozen. What was she saying? Was she saying that she was falling in love with him?

Surely not? Not after a week?

Sure, last night had been utterly incredible, but that wasn't love. Was it? It was passion. It was mutual understanding. It was compatibility. And, yes, he liked the way her smile lit up her whole face, turned mere prettiness into true beauty. He liked the way she was so cool and poised on the outside and yet fire and heat inside. He liked the way she stood up for what she believed in, even when it scared her to stand up and be counted.

But that wasn't love either, was it?

Love was messy and painful and loud and selfish. Love meant to hell with the rest of the world. Love meant operating on your terms, your way, no matter who got hurt. And when it went wrong you were left defenceless, revenge your only weapon.

He couldn't risk that. Couldn't be that vulnerable. There were other ways, better ways. It might sound cold: a timetable, a wish list and a criteria. But it was the key. The key to a quiet, successful life.

Although the truth was he had never met anyone who'd tempted him to more than a nice time. Anyone who'd made him want to make plans months in advance. Never met any woman he couldn't walk away from the moment things got difficult or messy.

Did that mean he was no better than his dad?

Maybe he was just a coward.

The silence had stretched wafer-thin. He needed to say something. He had no idea what to say.

'And how do you feel now?'

He held his breath. Would she make some kind of declaration? It was fine if she did. He knew it wasn't real. It would be the adrenaline from the evening, hormones still racing around after last night. If she had really been single, hadn't so much as dated in the last three years, then no wonder she was turned upside down by the attraction raging between them. It had discombobulated *him* after all.

He just needed to handle the situation with tact, with gentle skill.

Ellie leaned back in her seat. Her hands stilled. 'I feel ready to start living again. I am completely buzzed about the festival, about the work that lies ahead. And I'm not going to hide away any more. I'm going to go out there, start living, start dating again. Last night…yesterday…the whole week…' She trailed off. 'It's made me think. Think about who I want to be, *what* I want to be. And a lot of that is down to you. So, thank you.'

'You're welcome.'

Not a declaration. Not a grand passion. She wasn't in love with him. She was already thinking ahead. Thinking past him.

Which was great.

Wasn't it?

So why did he feel…well, *deflated*? Like a hot air balloon failing to lift off into the sky?

'No, I mean it. Last night was amazing. I didn't know I could feel like that, act like that. I'd never…'

She laughed. A low sound that penetrated deep into his bones, into his blood.

'I didn't think I would ever feel that free, that wanted. You showed me how it could be...how it *should* be.'

'It wasn't just me.' Max was uncomfortable cast in the role of Professor Higgins, and Ellie was certainly no Eliza Doolittle, ready for him to pluck, mould and shape. 'I think you were ready. I just provided the opportunity. Your hair, that dress...that's all you.'

The car had pulled up in front of the hotel. This was it. He would lead her back up to their suite and hopefully unzip that tight-fitting bodice, learn her body just a little bit more. Then tomorrow they would return to Cornwall and say their goodbyes. No hard feelings. Just warm memories. He would be free to sort out all the problems with DL Media and his parents; she would be free to start her new and more exciting life. A life he had helped her to kick start.

How very altruistic of him.

He couldn't have planned it better.

And he might feel a little hollow inside *now*,

but give him a week and Cornwall, London and Ellie Scott would all be distant memories. His life was complicated enough without adding long-distance relationships to it.

Besides, she didn't even want a relationship. Not with him. And that was absolutely fine.

Had she said something wrong?

Max's hand was around her waist, his fingers absentmindedly caressing the silky material of her dress, every touch sending sparks fizzing along her nerve-endings. The shock of winning, the champagne, the buzz of the whole evening and the last twenty minutes in such close proximity to Max had combined to create a perfect maelstrom of excitement—and she knew just the perfect way to work it out.

She tapped her foot, willing the lift on. As far as Ellie was concerned they couldn't get back to the privacy of their room soon enough.

But Max was distant, mentally if not physically, and had been for most of the journey. Was he thinking about work? Planning his next step?

The room tonight had twittered with gossip over DL Media's crisis. It had to be weighing on him.

She'd miss him. It had only been a week, but he had made such an impact on her life, crashing into it like a meteorite and shaking up everything she'd thought she knew, thought she wanted, thought she was. He'd challenged her, excited her, pushed her.

It was only natural that she would miss him. But his life was far, far away…a whole ocean away. And she hadn't even started to live hers yet.

It was time she did.

His arm remained around her waist as they walked the few short steps from the lift to the suite door, stayed there as he unlocked it and ushered her in.

The velvet cushions, gilt trimmings, opulent colours and brocade hangings hit her again with their over-the-top luxury. Ellie had somehow grown fond of their ridiculous suite. She had been reborn there. In less than forty-eight hours had made some huge changes. She just hoped that back in her own home she could keep the clarity and confidence she had gained here.

'Congratulations again. I thought we should celebrate.'

Max steered her over to the glass table. A complicated arrangement of lilies, roses and orchids dominated its surface, flanked by a bottle of vintage champagne chilling in an ice bucket, a lavish box of chocolates and a small purple tub.

'Champagne?'

Max followed her gaze. 'This is the hotel's Romance Package,' he murmured, his mouth close to her ear, his breath warm on her neck. 'Champagne, chocolate and massage oil.'

His eyes caught hers, full of meaning. Wherever he had been he was back. Back with clear intent.

He reached out and plucked the tub from the table. 'Sensual Jasmine with deep chocolate and sandalwood undertones. Feeling tense, Ellie?'

The promise in his voice shot straight through her.

Ellie shivered. 'A little.' It wasn't a lie.

'That's good. We can do something about that.'

Ellie swallowed, her eyes fixed on the small purple tub as he casually twisted it round and round in those oh, so capable fingers. 'We can?'

'Oh, yes. But you may want to disrobe first. I believe these oils can get rather...' His smile was pure wicked intent. 'Messy.'

'Messy?' Had she just squeaked?

'Oh, yeah. If you do it right, that is.'

She'd bet a year's takings that Max Loveday would do it right.

She stood there dry-mouthed as he picked up the bottle of champagne, deftly turning the wire and easing out the cork with practised ease.

'Well?' He poured champagne into one of the two flutes waiting by the bottle. 'What are you waiting for?'

Did he mean...? 'You want me to take my dress off?'

'Honey, I want you to take *everything* off. I have plans involving this...' He held up the champagne bottle. 'This...' He held up the massage oil. 'And your naked body. So come on: strip.'

Her breathing shallow, Ellie reached for the zip at the side of her dress. Her hands were clumsy, struggling to find the fastener, to draw it down the closely fitting bodice. Finally, *finally*, she pulled it down and let the dress fall away, standing in front of him in just her underwear.

At least it wasn't sensible this time. Tiny, silky wisps of black and red exposed far more than they concealed. It had taken all her resolve to put them on earlier, but hearing his sharp intake of breath, watching his eyes darken, filled her with a sensual power she had never felt before.

He might be issuing the demands, but she was the one in command.

She looked him clearly in the eye, didn't flinch or look away. 'Your turn. You said yourself things could get messy.'

Appreciation filled his face. 'You're playing with fire,' he warned as his hands moved to his tie. 'Be careful you don't get burned.'

'Oh, I'm counting on it.'

Ellie turned and walked into the master bedroom, head high, step confident even in those heels. She didn't need to turn around to see if he was following her. She knew he would be right behind her.

CHAPTER NINE

WHAT WAS THAT NOISE? An insistent buzz, as if an angry mosquito was trying to wake them up. An extremely loud, extremely angry mosquito.

Ellie reluctantly opened her eyes but it made no difference. The room was still dark. She put out her hand and encountered flesh; firm, warm flesh. Mmm… She ran her fingers appreciatively over Max's chest, learning him by heart once again.

Buzzzzz...

The mosquito had returned. Only it was no insect. Judging by the furiously flashing lights and the way it was dancing all over the bedside cabinet it was Ellie's phone making the racket.

Who on earth…?

Was it the shop?

Her heart began to speed up, skittering as frantically as her continuously buzzing phone as she pulled herself up, hands slipping on the rumpled sheets.

The buzzing stopped for one never-ending second, only to start up again almost immediately.

'What's that?' Max turned over, his voice thick with sleep.

'My phone. I don't know. It must be a wrong number.'

Please let it be a wrong number. Terrifying images ran through her mind in Technicolor glory: fire; flood, theft. All three…

Finally she got one trembling hand to the phone and pulled it over, pulling out the charging cable as she did so. Turning it over, she stared in disbelief at the name flashing up on the screen.

Mum.

What on earth…? She accepted the call with fingers too clumsy in their haste. 'Mum? Is everything all right?'

There was a pause, and then Ellie heard it. It was like being catapulted back in time. A painful, breathtaking blow as the years rolled back to the moment a policeman had knocked on the door and their lives had been irrevocably altered. That low keening, like an animal in severe distress.

She had hoped never to hear that noise again.

'Mum?'

'Ellie? Ellie? Oh, thank goodness, darling. It's Bill.' The words were garbled, breathless, but discernible.

Not now...please not now.

But even as her mind framed the words she pushed the thought away, shame swamping her. How could she be so selfish when catastrophe had torpedoed her mother's happiness once again?

And what *of* Bill? Big, blustering Bill? She barely knew him, not really, but he had supported her mother, loved her, given her a new life, a new beginning.

And if it was easier for her mother to cope without Ellie, the spitting image of her dad and so similar to her brother, a constant reminder of all that Marissa Scott had lost, then how could Ellie really blame her? Didn't she herself shy away from anything that reminded her of what she only now appreciated had been an extraordinarily perfect childhood?

'Mum, what's happened? Is he…?' She couldn't bring herself to utter the last word.

'He's had a heart attack. He's in Theatre now.'

Oh, thank God...thank God. 'Where are you? In Spain?'

She looked up, but Max was already firing up his laptop, phone at the ready. His poor PA was probably on hand to take his instructions. Relief shot through her. She knew instinctively that this time she wouldn't have to do it all alone. That he would sort out a flight, at least; probably cars, hotels…

'No, we're in Oakwood. Bill's daughter had a baby, so we came back for a visit.'

They were back in England, in close proximity to London. But they hadn't told her, hadn't suggested a trip to Cornwall, asked to see her. It wasn't the time for selfishness but Ellie couldn't help the sore thud of disappointment. Couldn't stop her mouth working as she swallowed back the huge, painful lump.

Knowing and understanding her mother's need for distance didn't stop it hurting.

But she had called now. She was in pain and she needed her daughter.

'I'm on my way. Give me a couple of hours. Do you need anything? Food? Clothes?'

'No, no. I'm okay. But, Ellie? *Hurry*, darling.'

Her face was pale and set, but there was strength in the pointed chin, in the dark, deeply shadowed eyes. A feeling of indomitability. Max had the sense Ellie had been here before, travelling through the night to support her mother.

'What about our things? Your hire car? You don't need to come with me.' They were the first words she had said since the town car had pulled up outside the hotel and they had exited the ornate lobby to find themselves in the strange, other-worldly pre-dawn of London.

Not quiet, London could never be completely still, but emptier, greyer, ghostlier. The chauffeur drove them at practised speed through the city streets, soon hitting suburbs as foreign and anonymous as every city's outskirts. Warehouses and concrete gave way to residential streets and then to fields and motorways.

'It's fine. Lydia will take care of it all.' He had already fired off several emails to his PA, and even though it was late night back in Hartford she had replied, was seamlessly sorting everything out. 'Our clothes will be packed up and sent back to Cornwall, and the car is getting picked up by the hire company.'

She nodded, but her attention was only half on him as she stared out of the window at the rapidly passing countryside. She was back in her usual grey. The scarlet dress was still lying on the floor of the sitting-room, a bright red puddle of silk. Make-up free, her hair pushed back behind her ears, the only hint that the evening had happened was the faint scent of jasmine on her skin; on his skin.

He shut his eyes, images of her passing through his mind like scenes from a film. Her body, long, slender, slick with oil, as his hands moved firmly over silken skin.

'What about work? DL needs you.' Her voice was toneless.

He opened his eyes, the last remnants of the night before fading away. *Not the time or place,* he scolded himself. 'It's fine. Let's see what your mother needs and I can worry about DL later. The hospital will have WiFi, won't it?'

She nodded. 'I guess. It's a long time since I've been there. Not since Dad and Phil...' Her voice trailed off.

'Your mom's back in your old home town?'

No wonder she looked so haunted.

'For fourteen years I thought it was the most perfect place in the world.' Her voice was wistful. 'I danced. Did you know that?'

'No, but I should have guessed.' Of course she had danced. That long, toned slenderness was a dancer's legacy.

'I danced, played in the orchestra and was a member of the drama society. Phil played rugby and swam. We were like a family from an advertisement, with the golden Labrador to match.'

She turned towards him, her chin propped in her hand, her eyes far away.

'At weekends we'd all bike out for picnics in the countryside and then we'd pile on the sofa for family film and pizza night. I guess Mum and Dad must have argued, and I know Phil and I did, but when I look back it's like it's painted in soft gold. Always summer, always laughter. And then it all went wrong…' Her voice trailed off.

'The car accident.'

She nodded. 'Mum blamed herself. Dad had been travelling and was jetlagged, but she hated driving on ice so she persuaded him to pick Phil up from a swim meet. It was a drunk driver. The police said there was nothing Dad could have done. But Mum always thought if he hadn't been so tired…' She blinked, and there was a shimmering behind the long lashes.

Max's chest ached with the need to make it all right. But how could he? How could anybody?

'It must have been terrible.'

'I think that's why Mum had a breakdown. So she didn't have to face the guilt. But I had to face it all: insurance, funeral-arranging, keeping the house going. I gave up dance, drama, friends, my dreams. There was school, there was Mum and there were books—the only escape from how grey my life had become.'

'But you got away.'

A new town, a new life. The loneliness of that

life was beginning to make a twisted kind of sense to him. Could he say the same for his own choices?

Ellie nodded. 'It took a while. When I finished school I was supposed to go to university, but I couldn't see how she would cope without me and I was too proud to ask for help. Then Mum met Bill at her support group and suddenly she didn't need me any more. Worse, it was as if she couldn't bear to see me...like I made her feel guilty. She went from not being able to cope without me to not wanting to be near me. I lost everything all over again.'

Max didn't know what to say. Was there anything he *could* say? Anything that could wipe away over ten years of loneliness and grief?

He reached out instead, took her cold, still hand in his.

Ellie clung on, glad of the tactile comfort. His hands were warm, anchoring her to the here and now.

'What did you do then? Is that when you got engaged?'

The chill enveloping her deepened. *Engaged.* It was such happy word. It conjured up roses and diamonds and champagne. She hadn't experienced any of those things. Just an ornate ring that had belonged to Simon's grandmother: an ugly Victorian emerald that she had never dared tell him she disliked.

Simon was her secret shame, her weakness. She had never been able to tell anyone the whole story before. But there was a strength in Max's touch, in his voice, that made her want to lean in, to rest her burden on his broad shoulders. Just for a while.

She took a deep breath. She had said so much already…would a little more hurt? 'I hadn't seen much of my friends out of school, but it was still a shock when they went to university. So I got a job at the solicitors where my father had worked, just to get out of the house. Everyone there was a lot older, and I knew, of course, that they had only employed me to be kind.'

'Simon…'

She waited for the usual thump in her chest, the twist of dread to strike her as she said his name. But there was nothing. It was just a word, an old ghost with no way to harm her. Not if she didn't allow it.

Ellie carried on, her voice stronger. 'Simon was the only person there who didn't talk to me like I was a child. After the first couple of weeks I had a huge crush on him.' She shook her head, a bitter taste coating her mouth at the memory of her naïve younger self. 'He knew, of course. Enjoyed it and encouraged it, I think.'

She fell silent for a moment, the memory hitting her hard. Her mother's happiness—one she couldn't share. The resentment she hadn't been able to bring herself to acknowledge because it was so petty and mean; resentment that she had given up her childhood and future for her mother and now *she* was the one being left behind. And the coldness of her isolation. The dawning knowledge that her mother not only no longer needed her but somehow no longer wanted her.

Ellie shivered and Max put an arm around her, pulling her in close, holding her against his warm strength.

She turned into his comforting embrace, her

arms slipping around him, allowing herself the luxury of leaning on him, *into* him, just this once. She inhaled deep, that smell of pine and salt, of sea and fresh air that clung to him even after two days in London.

'Looking back now, I can see that I was just desperate to feel loved, cared for. Simon sensed it, I think…my indecision, my loneliness…and he made his move.'

Her mouth twisted.

'He was very clever. One moment he would flatter me, make me feel like the most desirable woman alive. The next he would tease me, treat me like a silly schoolgirl. He'd stand me up and then turn up to whisk me away on an impossibly romantic date. I never knew where I stood. As he intended.'

She swallowed.

'And right from the start I tried to be what he wanted. To wear my hair the way he liked, dress in a way he approved of. He never actually said anything—but he would get this *look*, you know? This terribly disappointed look. Sometimes he would stop speaking to me altogether, not contact me if I really displeased him, and I would never know why. I'd have to figure it out. I used to sit alone in the empty house and cry, stare at my phone willing him to text me. When he finally spoke to me I'd be so relieved I would promise myself I would never upset him again. I learned what was expected of me, what would make him smile in approval. My food, my clothes, the books I read, the films I watched—all guided by him. I thought I was in love. That he protected me, cared for me.'

Max's whole body was rigid, and when she peeped over she saw a muscle beating in his cheek. His fingers gripped hers tightly, almost painful in their intensity.

'When Mum told me she was moving to Spain with Bill, selling the house, Simon came to the rescue; my knight in shining armour. He asked why didn't I move in, and I couldn't think of a single reason not to.'

She laced her fingers through Max's.

'It all happened so slowly. First he suggested I give up my job so that I could study. But then he found a hundred reasons for me to delay starting a course and I agreed. Because, you see, I thought he was protecting me.'

She swallowed again.

'I don't know when it dawned on me that I didn't have a single thing to call my own. Not for a long time. I forgot that it wasn't normal to be terrified in case you said the wrong thing, in case the house wasn't neat enough, the dishes tidied away, the bed made perfectly, my hair and clothes perfect. I didn't realise for a long time that I could barely breathe, that I was terrified of his displeasure, that just one frown could crush me.

'Because the worst thing of all,' her voice was low now, as she admitted the part that shamed her most. 'The worst thing of all is that when he smiled, when I got it right, I was elated. So that's what I strived for. I looked right, said the right things. When he was happy I was happy. I thought I was so very happy.'

She blinked, almost shocked to feel the wetness on her eyelashes.

'I don't know when I first realised that living in fear wasn't normal. Never relaxing, always worrying, never knowing what would set him off.

He told me time and time again how worthless I was, how lucky I was to have him, and after a while I believed him.'

Because how could a girl with nothing be worth anything? Even her own mother had discarded her like an unwanted toy.

'When he wanted to he could be the sweetest, most tender person in the world. And I craved it. I thought it must be my fault that he was angry so often. He told me it was my fault.'

Max swallowed, his voice thick as he spoke. 'So what happened?'

'It wasn't one argument or one incident. It just crept up on me that I was desperately unhappy, and that every time someone mentioned the wedding I felt as if I was being bricked up alive. And as I got more and more scared he got more and more controlling. He wanted to know where I was every hour, would be angry if he phoned home and I didn't answer. He went through my receipts, looking for goodness knows what. One day I realised that I was afraid. I think it was the first time I'd allowed myself to think like that. But once I had it was as if a door had opened and I couldn't shut it again. So I just left. Jumped on a train to Cornwall. For six months I looked over my shoulder all the time, dreading seeing him there—and yet hoping he loved me enough to track me down. To find me.'

It was out. Every last sordid detail.

Would Max judge her? He couldn't judge her any more than she'd judged herself.

Ellie turned apprehensive eyes to him, dreading the judgement she expected to see in his face. His hands tightened on hers as he looked down at her, his mouth set, his eyes hard. But not with anger directed at her, no. Compassion softened the grim lines of his face.

'Look at you now, Ellie. Just look what you've become. You didn't let the jerk stop you. Delay you, maybe, but not stop you. You're strong, independent, successful, compassionate. You should be so proud of yourself.'

Proud? Not ashamed? Strong? Not weak? Was that really, truly what he saw?

Ellie didn't move for one long moment but then she fell against him with a gulp, tears spilling down her face, her chest heaving with the sobs she had held back for far too long.

Slipping an arm around her, Max pulled her in close, let her lean on him, let his shirt absorb her tears, his shoulders absorb her pain. He held her close, rubbed her back and kissed the top of her head as the car continued to drive through the gloom and Ellie cried it all out.

Her head ached, her throat ached, her eyes ached. In fact there wasn't a part of her that didn't hurt in one way or another. Not in the languorous way she had ached yesterday morning, with that sated, sensual feeling, but a much more painful sensation, as if she had been ripped apart and clumsily glued back together, cracks and dents and all.

Max's hand was still on hers, tethering her to the here and now, keeping her grounded. When had she ever cried like that before? She didn't think she ever had. At first she had been too numb and then? Then she had had to keep it together. One of them had to.

'Are you angry with her?' Max's voice stirred the silence.

'Sorry?'

'Your mother.' He shook his head. 'I mean, I'm pretty furious with *my* mother, for being so greedy and stubborn, and I am absolutely filled with rage against my dad for—well, for pretty much everything. But none of it is about me. I could walk away tomorrow, I guess, and leave them to it. Heck, maybe I should. Difference is I'm an adult. But you? You were just a kid. She made you be the grown-up, and then when you needed her she wasn't there.'

Ellie opened her mouth, ready to defend her mother—and herself. But the words wouldn't come. 'I…'

'It's okay, you know. You're allowed to be angry. It doesn't make you bad. It just makes you human.'

Anger? Was that what she felt? That tightening in her chest, the way her fingernails bit into her palms whenever she got a breezy, brief email from her mother?

Brief, breezy. The bare minimum of contact.

And when Ellie had fled, needing somewhere to hide out and recover, her mother hadn't been there for her. Hadn't wanted her. Hadn't known or cared that her daughter was trapped in a vicious relationship. What kind of woman left her eighteen-year-old daughter alone with a much older man she hardly knew?

'I *am* angry. So angry.' The words were almost a whisper. 'That she left me to deal with it all. That she made me be the grown-up when I wasn't ready. That she let me give up university for her. That she just left me...' Her voice was rising in volume and intensity and she stopped, shocked by the shaking fury in it.

His hand tightened on hers. 'How did you feel then?'

Ellie tried never to think about that particular time, that last betrayal. No wonder, when dragging it all up cut deeply all over again. 'Lost,' she admitted. 'I think, I wonder if she hadn't gone just then, if things might have been different. If I might have gone to university, not got engaged.'

She stopped.

'But I was an adult by then,' she said instead. 'I made my choices just as she made hers. I can't blame her. I can't blame anyone but myself.'

'No, you were still a child. You have nothing to regret, Ellie. Nothing at all.'

Neither of them spoke then, but Max continued to hold her hand, his thumb caressing the back of her hand with sure movements as the car took them through increasingly familiar countryside, finally entering the outskirts of the town where Ellie had been born.

She was finding it increasingly hard to get her breath, and her stomach was clenching as they entered the hospital car park.

'Hey.' Max gave her a reassuring smile. 'It's fine. You're not alone. Not this time.'

Ellie tried to smile back but she couldn't make her muscles obey. Right now she wasn't alone—but next week he would be gone, and she would be back to square one. On her own.

Somehow Max Loveday had slipped through all her defences and shown her just what a sham her life was. Safe? Sure. Protected? Absolutely. Hardworking and honest? Maybe. But true? No. Hiding away, not having fun, trusting no one… That wasn't true to the legacy of love and happiness her father and brother had left her, that Demelza Loveday had bequeathed to her.

Max or no Max, Ellie had to find a way to start living again.

If she could only work out where to start.

CHAPTER TEN

THE CORRIDORS WERE the same off-white, the floor the same hard-wearing highly polished tiles, the smell the same: antiseptic crossed with boiled vegetables. She might be fourteen again, hurrying down the corridor, following in her mother's frantic footsteps.

But this time Max's hand was on her arm: a quiet, tacit support. Five days ago she hadn't been able to wait to see the back of Max Loveday. Today she was grateful he was here at all.

It was as if her godmother was still looking out for her, even after her death.

'Here we are. Ward Six.'

Max would have walked straight in, but Ellie came to an abrupt halt.

'I just need a moment.'

'Sure. Take as long as you need.' He was wearing jeans with the tuxedo shirt from the night before: an incongruous mix that he somehow managed to carry off. Maybe the early-morning stubble and ruffled hair helped. Or maybe it was his innate confidence.

Or it could be the surroundings. These corridors must have seen people turn up in everything from pyjamas to ballgowns. Last time she had pulled on grey tracksuit bottoms and an old football shirt of her brother's. She could see it as if it were yesterday, feel the smooth nylon of the shirt, hear the slopping of the flip-flops she had grabbed, forgetting about the snow outside.

Ellie inhaled, a long, slow breath, filling her chest with air, with oxygen, with courage. And then she pushed open the door and walked into the ward's waiting room.

Again memories assailed her. Could they be the same industrial padded chairs? The same leaflets on the noticeboard? The same water-cooler with no cups anywhere to be seen? The same tired potted plant?

Only the people were different.

She half recognised Bill's family from the pitifully few occasions when they had met; his daughter, a few years older than Ellie, now cradling a baby. His brother, as tall and thickset as Bill, his sister, red-eyed and staring into space.

And pacing up and down like a caged wild animal, just as she had the last time, was her mother. A little older, her skin far more tanned, her hair blonder, a little plumper, but still recognisably, indisputably Marissa Scott.

She turned as Ellie pushed the door open and Ellie stood still for a moment, wary, as if they were strangers. She had to speak, to break the silence.

'Hi, Mum.'

It wasn't enough, and yet it was all she had. But as her mother broke into a trot and ran across the room to enfold her in her arms Ellie realised that maybe, just maybe, it was enough after all.

'What a day.' Max sat back in the uncomfortable cafeteria chair and looked down at the plate of pale fried food in front of him. He poked suspiciously at the peas, soggy and a nasty yellowish green. 'Do you think there is actually *any* nutritional value in this?'

'Not an iota.' Ellie had wisely eschewed the fish and chips and gone for a salad. 'Hospital food is like school food: something to be endured.'

Max tried not to think too longingly of the food at his expensive private school. 'We should have gone out.'

'Maybe I should have insisted you leave earlier. You didn't have to stay all day. Did you get any work done?'

'Some,' Max admitted.

He knew Ellie had had an agonising day, waiting with her overwrought mother for Bill to come out of surgery, and that his day couldn't compare—but it had been no walk in the park. He had spent the day delving deeply into DL Media's accounts and his excavations hadn't uncovered any gold. All he had found was a big pit that was getting deeper by the day.

'There are some difficult decisions to make when I get back.'

His last four words seemed to hang in the air.

'I do appreciate you taking so much time out of your schedule for me. I know you were hoping to spend more time in London.' Ellie's head was bent and she was poking unenthusiastically at her salad.

'Ellie, it's nothing. And it's not as if I'm not in contact with the London office every day.' For once Max didn't want to talk about work—or dwell on how little time he had left in the UK. 'How's Bill?'

'Out of surgery. And the doctors seem pleased.'

'And your mother?'

'Surprisingly okay.' Her cheeks flushed. 'Well enough to ask who you are.'

He raised an eyebrow. 'What did you tell her?'

Her eyes lowered. 'That we work together.'

'Okay.'

He speared a soggy chip and then laid his fork down. He wasn't hungry after all. He looked around. The room was half full: a few patients well enough to get up and walk about, harassed-looking staff shovelling food in as quickly and efficiently as engines refuelling. And friends and relatives, many with shell-shocked faces.

He really didn't want to spend much more time

here, and neither should Ellie. Her eyes were deeply shadowed, her face white with tiredness.

'What do you want to do? Are you planning to stay with your mother for a few days?'

He was surprised at how much he wanted her to say no. If she didn't return to Trengarth with him today would he see her again this trip?

Or at all.

She shook her head and unexpected relief flooded through him.

'Part of me feels like I should, but there's nowhere for me to stay and Bill's family are looking after Mum. If there was any suggestion he was still in danger of course I would... No, I need to get back to the shop. There's no reason for me to hang around. Thanks for bringing me. Max.' Her eyes met his. 'For everything.'

'Any time.' He meant it too. There had been no thought in the early morning of walking away, of putting her into a car and returning to his own world. 'Do you want to find a hotel for the night or get straight off? I could get us a car in an hour, although we wouldn't get back to Cornwall until the early morning.'

She chewed her lip, her eyes flickering as she thought. ‘Is it bad that I just want to go home?’

‘Not at all. It’s been a long day. I’ll get one ordered. We can sleep in the car if we need to. Although…’ He looked at his untouched plate and then at hers. ‘We may want to stop for some real food first.’

‘That sounds good. I’ll go and sit with Mum for a bit longer.’

‘I’ll fetch you when the car gets here.’

She didn’t move straight away. She just sat, looking as if there was something she wanted to say. Max waited, but she didn’t speak, just gave him a tremulous smile as she pushed her chair back and walked slowly out of the cafeteria.

The car rolled smoothly through the night-dark moor. Clouds blocked the stars, and as Max stared out of the window all he could see was his own reflection. Unsmiling, contemplative. Angry.

Max Loveday wasn’t a violent man. His battles were in the boardroom, in sales figures and profits. But tonight his blood ran hot. All he could think about was asking the driver to turn back to Oakwood, so that he could find Ellie's ex and make him wish he had never set eyes on her.

And he'd ask her mother just exactly what she had been thinking when she had allowed her teenage daughter to become the adult. When she had left that daughter alone with nowhere to turn except to an emotionally abusive and controlling man.

Only Ellie didn't want or need him to fight her battles, even though all he wanted was to ride into the lists for her, to pull on a helmet and grab a sword and rush into battle for her honour.

And to teach that scoundrel a lesson.

His lips tightened. He hadn't felt this out of control, this primal, in years. His instincts were screaming at him to protect, to avenge.

This was exactly what he wanted to avoid. This kind of messy, hot-headed emotion, pulling and pushing him away from his goals, from his plans. Love—violent, needy love—was to blame for it all. Grieving love, causing Ellie's mother's breakdown. Twisted love, creating a hellish trap for Ellie.

His hands curled into fists. It wasn't love affecting his judgement right now. It was lust and liking, respect and admiration. But it was still dangerous.

Thank goodness he would be on his way home in just a few days.

Just a few days…

It wasn't long enough.

It was far too long. A dangerously long time.

He glanced over at Ellie. She was curled up on the seat next to him, sleeping as the car wound its way through the tiny lanes that would take them back to Trengarth. Visibly yawning as they'd finished their excellent pub dinner, Ellie hadn't taken long to fall asleep once they'd returned to the car. Max wasn't surprised; she'd exorcised all her ghosts in one day. There was bound to be a price, both physically and mentally. Better she sleep it off.

What about him? Would he be able to exorcise his own ghosts?

Max shifted in his seat, wishing he could get comfortable. He supposed the question was did he even want to? After all, hadn't they kept him safe? But he had to admit his careful planning, his definition of a suitable partner, didn't fill him with the same quiet satisfaction it had used to.

He sighed, changing position once again. The whole point of getting a driver to take them all the way back to Trengarth had been so they could rest, but Max was unable to switch off. He envied the slow, even sound of Ellie's breath.

It would have been better for him to have driven himself, forced to concentrate on the road ahead rather than sit here in the dark with the same thoughts running through his mind over and over on a loop.

'Where now, sir?'

The driver was turning down the coastal road that led directly to the village.

'Should I drop the lady off first?'

They were back.

London, the suite, playing at tourists—it was all over. He should see Ellie home and that would be an end to it, *should* be an end to it. Only she was so tired. And so alone.

'No.' Max made a sudden decision. Ellie would be tired, emotionally wrung out when she came to. She might need him. And after all he had bedrooms to spare. 'Both of us to The Round House, please.'

It was less than five minutes before the car pulled in through the gates and came to a smooth stop on the circular driveway. The outside light came on as they passed it, and the orange glow cast an otherworldly light over the still slumbering Ellie.

Max eyed her. She was thin, sure, and couldn't weigh too much. How easy would it be to get her out of the car and upstairs without waking her?

Not that easy.

But she looked so peaceful he didn't want to disturb her.

He opened the car door as quietly as he could, hoping to give her just a few seconds more, but she stirred as the door clicked open.

'Where are we?' Her voice was groggy.

Max glanced over. Her hair was mussed, her eyes still half shut.

'At The Round House. It's so late I thought we could both stay here tonight. I can make up a bed for you, if you prefer.'

'No need. I don't mind sharing.' She yawned: an impossibly long sound. 'I should walk home. It's not far, but I don't think I'd make it. I'd probably fall asleep by the side of the road and have to trust that the local rabbits and sparrows would cover me with leaves.'

'Very picturesque, but if you could make do with sheets and a mattress it might be easier.'

'Okay, if you insist.' She yawned again and allowed him to help her out of the car, leaning against him as she staggered upright.

'Come on, Sleeping Beauty, let's go in.'

Max had only stayed a few nights in The Round House, occupied it for less than a week, and yet somehow it felt like coming home.

Walking in, dropping his wallet and keys in the glass bowl on the hallway table, kicking his shoes off by the hat stand: they all felt like actions honed by years of automatic practice. And the house welcomed him back. A sigh seemed to ripple through it, one of contentment. All was right in its world.

He didn't have this sense of rightness in his own apartment. All glass and chrome and space, city views, personal gym, residents' pool on site, it was the perfect bachelor pad. But when he was there he didn't fall asleep listening to the waves crashing on the beach below. His apartment was luxurious, convenient, easy—but it didn't have family history steeped into every cornice. Sure, he could move some of the old family possessions, the pictures, the barometer, over to Hartford. But they wouldn't belong there.

They belonged here.

'Do you need anything?'

The question was automatic but he wasn't sure he could help if she did. The kitchen had been bare when he'd arrived, and he'd stocked it with little more than coffee, milk and some nachos.

Luckily Ellie shook her head. 'Just bed.'

'I'm in the guest suite.' He started to lead the way up the wide staircase. 'It didn't feel right, moving into my great-aunt's rooms.'

'That's understandable. Besides, I can't see you as a rose wallpaper kind of guy.'

'It *is* very floral,' he agreed. 'But I'm secure enough in my masculinity to cope with pink roses.'

She raised her eyebrows. '*There's* a claim.'

Max slid his arm around her waist, his steps matching hers as they trod wearily up the stairs. Yet some of that weariness fell away as he touched her.

'I don't make claims. I make statements.'

Ellie had reached the landing half a step ahead. She turned to him, stepping into his embrace, her own arms encircling his waist, warm hands burrowing underneath his T-shirt. His skin tingled where she touched: a million tiny explosions as his nerve-endings reacted to the skin-on-skin contact.

'I may need you to verify that statement.'

She looked up at him, her face serious except for that dimple tugging at the corner of her mouth. He bent his head, needing to taste the little dip in her skin. He felt her shiver against him as his tongue dipped out and sampled her.

'I'm at your service.' He kissed the dimple again, inhaling her sweet, drowsy scent as he did so. 'How exactly would you like me to verify it?' He kissed his way down her jawline, pausing at her neck. 'Any requests?'

Her hands clenched at his waist. 'Anything.'

'Anything?' He slid his hands up under her top, over her ribs to the soft fullness above.

Ellie gasped. 'Anything. Just don't stop.'

'Oh, I won't, honey. Not until you ask me to.'

He walked her backwards towards the bedroom door, his hands continuing to move upwards millimetre by millimetre.

'It's only three in the morning. We've got the rest of the night.'

He couldn't, *wouldn't* think beyond that. Not now. Not when his hands were caressing her, his lips tasting her. When the scent of her was all around him.

There were decisions to be made, places to go and a world to conquer. But it could wait until the morning.

The sun would be up in just a couple of hours, but they still had tonight and Max was going to make the most of every single second.

The sun was shining in through the half-opened curtains, casting a warm golden glow onto the bed. Ellie sighed and pulled at the sheet as she turned into the gentle heat, gloriously aware that at that very second everything was all right with the world.

Except... Except was she waking up alone again? Like some Greek nymph fated never to see her lover in the light of day?

Ellie pulled herself upright and tried to work out the time. There was no clock in the room, and her phone was dead, but judging by the brightness of the sun it had to be late morning if not afternoon.

She should really get up. Check on her shop. Head back to reality. Only she was so comfortable. Reality could wait just a little longer.

'Morning, sleepyhead. Or should that be afternoon?'

Max was lounging against the door, holding something that Ellie devoutly hoped was a cup of coffee.

'I thought you were going to sleep the day away.'

'How long have you been up?' She held her hand out for the coffee and inhaled greedily, wrapping her hands around the hot mug. 'I missed you.' She allowed her hand to fall invitingly to the empty space by her side, the sheet to slip a little lower.

'No rest for the wicked. Duty called.'

He wasn't meeting her eye, and he didn't sit by her or even slide his gaze appreciatively over her body.

The message was clear. Playtime was over. Well, she had known the deal from the start. Any disappointment was simply her due payment for the unexpected fun. Back to reality with the proverbial bump.

No wonder it stung a little.

'My solicitor wants to look at the share papers in detail. He doesn't trust the scan I sent him, so it looks like I might be heading back earlier than I expected. Don't worry about the festival, though. I've asked our marketing guys to give you a hand, and my PA can do whatever you need her to do. I've emailed you all the details.'

Max sounded offhand: more like the business partner she had been expecting him to be than the understanding companion of the last few days.

'Very efficient,' Ellie said drily. 'You *have* been

busy. In that case I'd better get off. I don't want to hold you up. When are you flying out?'

That was good. Her voice was level, with no outward sign that she felt as if she'd been kicked in the stomach.

Of course she'd known this wasn't for ever… hadn't been expecting more than a few more days. Only she had been looking forward to those few more days. Looking forward to discovering more about him, discovering more about herself, about who she could be with a little support and an absence of fear.

Well, she would have to carry on that discovery alone.

'Tomorrow. I've a car booked for ten tomorrow morning.'

His eyes caught hers then, and there was a hint of an apology in the caramel depths, along with something else. A barrier. He was moving on, moving away. Oh, so politely, but oh, so steadily.

Ellie knew that she should try and get up, but she was suddenly and overwhelmingly self-conscious. Her clothes were heaped on a chair at the other side of the room and she couldn't, absolutely *couldn't* get up and walk across there stark naked. Maybe she could have if the other Max had been here. The Max who couldn't keep his eyes off her. The Max who made her feel infinitely precious and yet incredibly strong, like a rare stone ready to be polished into something unique.

But this Max was a stranger, and she didn't want him to see her in all her vulnerability.

'Thanks for the coffee but, really, don't let me keep you. We both have heaps to do. Maybe I'll see you before you leave. Come down to the shop if you have a chance. I'll find you a book for the plane.'

She could be polite and businesslike too.

'Thanks, that would be good.' Max stepped back towards the door. 'Not that I'll have a chance to read for pleasure. I'll be...'

'Busy,' she finished for him. 'Back to all work and no play, Max?'

He flushed, a hint of red high on the tanned cheekbones. 'Yes.'

Shame shot through her at his quiet acceptance. 'I'm sorry. I know you have to go. I know how difficult things are.' She smiled. 'I guess I've got used to you being around.'

The colour had left his cheeks and he smiled back, the familiar warmth creeping back into his eyes. 'I've got used to *being* around. I'll miss it here.'

And me? she wanted to ask. *Will you miss me?* But her mouth wouldn't form the words; she wasn't entirely sure what she wanted the answer to be.

He was watching her now with his old intentness, the expression that made her simultaneously want to pull the sheet right up to her chin and let it fall all the way down.

'I guess I *could* take a few hours off today. I never did get round to taking a boat out. Do you have to get back to the shop, Ellie?'

Yes. No. Things were confusing enough already. Maybe she would be better off saying her goodbyes now and putting some much needed distance between them. But what could a few more hours hurt? The end line was firmly drawn in the sand. The countdown to the final hour had begun.

'They're not expecting me back till this evening. Mrs T has the shop well in hand, I'm sure.'

'Good.' He pushed away from the doorway and advanced on her, intent clear and hot in his eyes. 'In a couple of hours we should get a picnic, and then I'll show you that the sea is for more than watching. Ready to try something new, Ellie?'

He *was* talking about sailing, wasn't he? Shivers ran hot down her body.

'In a couple of hours?'

The sheet fell a little more and this time he noticed, his eyes scorching gold as they traced their way down her body.

'A couple of hours,' he agreed. 'I haven't said good morning to you properly yet, or good afternoon. In fact I may need to work my way right through to good evening…'

'Well,' she said, as primly as it was possible to be when lying barely covered by a sheet, her body trembling with anticipation, 'we wouldn't want to forget our manners, now, would we?'

'Absolutely not.' He was by her side, his eyes fixed on hers as he began to slowly unbutton his shirt. 'Manners are very important. Want me to show you?'

She nodded, her gaze skimming the defined hardness of his chest, moving lower down to where he was just beginning to unfasten his jeans.

'Yes. Yes, please, Max. Show me everything.'

CHAPTER ELEVEN

'ARE YOU SURE you've got everything?'

Ellie hadn't intended to come and see Max off. She hadn't intended to stay with him all last night, or to wake up in his arms this morning. She had intended a civilised kiss on the cheek before turning away, as if she didn't much care whether he stayed or went.

And yet here she was. She hated goodbyes as a matter of course, but this one was proving particularly unbearable. The problem with never dating, never having had a casual relationship in her life, was that she had no idea how to act now their time was coming to an end.

Should she hug him? Kiss his cheek? Kiss him properly? Shake his hand? High-five him? All of the above? Grab him and never let him go?

That wasn't in their unwritten agreement.

Max picked up his small holdall, hefting the

weight experimentally. 'I think so. I didn't actually buy much while I was here, and I packed light anyway.'

'You nearly bought a boat.'

'But I wasn't planning to check that in as hand luggage. Even first class might have had something to say about that.'

'They probably wouldn't have been best pleased.' Ellie rummaged in her bag and pulled out a gold-embossed paper bag. 'Have you got room for this? I owe you a souvenir, remember?'

He eyed the bag nervously. 'It's not a trick snake, is it?'

'No.' She bit her lip, keeping back her smile with some difficulty. 'Open it when you get home.'

'That bad, huh?'

'You have no idea.'

She handed him another bag: one of the striped paper bags she used at the shop.

'Here. I know you're planning to work solidly for the next twenty-four hours, but just in case your eyes tire of spreadsheets…'

He opened the bag and slid the hardback book out. '*Tales of Cornwall*? It's lovely. Thanks, Ellie.'

'I figured you should know a little about your ancestral folk.'

He was flicking through it, pausing at some of the full-colour illustrations. 'It's a very thoughtful gift.' He looked at her, his brow crinkled. 'I don't have anything for you. I'm sorry.'

'That's okay. I wasn't expecting anything.' She swallowed, her throat unexpectedly full. 'Just promise me you won't sell the house to anyone who doesn't love it.'

'I'd keep it if I could, but you said it yourself, Ellie. The village doesn't need any more absentee owners, jetting in for two weeks in the summer. I'll make sure I only sell it to a family who want to live here all year round.'

'A book-loving family?'

'Of course. What about you, Ellie? Are you going to be okay?'

His face was serious and the concern in his voice made her hands clench a little. It wasn't that she didn't appreciate it; it was nice that someone cared even a little. But she didn't want that kind of concern from Max.

Her preference would be for the scorching looks that turned her knees to melting chocolate—made her whole body liquefy. But she'd even take his scornful mistrust. That at least had treated her as an equal, not like something fragile.

'Yes. I have your PA's email, and I promise to call DL's London office if I need advice or help.'

'That's not what I meant. Are you sure this is what you want?'

Ellie's heart thumped painfully. What did he mean? Was he offering to stay? For her to go with him? For some kind of tomorrow beyond these two weeks? Her palms felt clammy as her pulse began to race. What would she say? What *did* she want?

'Am I sure about what?'

'This...' He swept his arm dismissively in an arc, pushing away Trengarth, the sea, the view. 'It's pretty, Ellie. But is it enough? One shop? One festival? You were amazing at the weekend: passionate, knowledgeable, brilliant. You told me you dreamt once of a life in London, in publishing. Are you really content to settle for *this*?'

It was the hint of contempt in his voice as he said 'this' that really hit her. Was that what he thought? Of her? Of Trengarth? Of everything she valued? That they weren't big enough? Not important enough?

'It's okay, Max. You can head back to your important job in the big city without worrying about me. I *am* happy and *I am fine*.'

The last three words came out slightly more vehemently than she'd meant them to and Max took a step back, his eyes widened in surprise.

'Whoa, what does *that* mean?'

'It means you don't have to add me to the list of things that Max Loveday has to sort out. I like my life, Max. I like my shop. I love my village. We don't all need to be at the very top. We don't all need to save the world.'

Confusion warred with anger in his eyes. 'I'm not trying to save the world.'

'No?'

She put her hands on her hips and glared at him. She wanted him to look as if he might miss her, darn it. To look as if not holding her, kissing her, touching her might actually cause him some discomfort. As if he wanted to pull her into bed—not tell her everything that was wrong with her life, according to the gospel of Max Loveday.

'No.'

Good intentions be damned. She was going to have to say something.

'When you came here you accused me of being some kind of con artist. Now you tell me I'm wasting my life. Things aren't that black and white, Max. Life is richer and more complicated than your narrow definition of success. Look at your dad and his girlfriend. Have you considered that maybe, just maybe, they really are in love?'

His mouth tightened. 'I don't doubt that they *believe* that.'

'How will you know if you don't give them a chance? You carry responsibility for your parents, for the whole of DL, for your grandfather's dreams. What about you, Max? What do *you* want?'

'You know what I want.'

Yes, she did. And she wasn't anywhere on that list.

'For DL Media to work like clockwork, your parents to behave, and to find your perfect wife at the perfect time? I have news for you, Max. Life isn't that simple. Life is emotional and messy and demanding, and you can't hide behind spread-sheets for ever. When you find her, this right woman at the right time to make the perfect life with, she's going to have her own chips and flaws. Her own desires and needs.'

'I know that.' His face was white under the tan, his eyes hard.

'*Do* you?'

Ellie stepped forward and put her hand on his arm, relieved when he didn't try and shake her off.

'You have helped me so much this last week. Helped me confront the past, helped me move on. I feel free, reborn. But it's down to me now. It's always been down to me. To move on or to lock myself away. *My* choice. Just like your parents can make their own choices. And you. *You* can choose too, you know.'

'I have chosen, Ellie. I choose to honour my commitments. I choose to live and dream big, to keep pushing. There's nothing wrong with that.'

'I thought I was the one who was too scared to reach out.' She looked at him, *really* at him, trying to see through to the closely guarded heart of him. 'But you're just as bad. I hope you find what you're looking for, Max. I hope it's worth it.'

He covered her hand with his and squeezed, the rigid look fading from his face. 'It will be. Same to you. Dream big, Ellie.'

'I'll try.'

His hand was warm, comforting over hers. She might not need him but the uncomfortable truth was that she did *want* him. Her bed was going to feel larger than it had used to, her walks on the beach a little more solitary. But that was fine. She had the festival to plan. A social life to start.

She stood on her tiptoes and kissed his lightly stubbled cheek, breathing him in one last time. 'You'd better get going. Safe flight, Max.'

'See you around, honey.'

'Yes.' She paused, then stepped closer, tiptoeing up towards him again. This time she touched her lips to his…a brief caress. 'Bye.'

And she turned and walked away, ignoring the whisper in her heart telling her to turn round and ask him to stay.

What could she offer him here in Cornwall? Only herself. And that would never be enough.

When had Max's office become so confining? Oh, he still had views over downtown Hartford, still had room to pace, a huge desk, a comfortable yet imposing chair. But somehow his horizons felt strangely limiting.

Even though he could walk out now, if he wanted to. Could organise a meeting in Sydney or Paris or Prague and be on a plane within hours.

Be in London within hours.

Max picked up the snow globe that now stood right next to his laptop dock: a penguin balanced on an iceberg encased in a glass bauble. He hadn't known what to expect when Ellie had given him the paper bag but it certainly hadn't been this. Delicate, intricate, mesmerising.

Like its giver.

He shook it, watching the tiny flakes fall on to the miniature black and white bird, turning the arctic scene into a fairytale. It *had* been a fairytale. For just a few days. But he was back in reality now.

Back in reality and ridiculously restless.

He wasn't sleeping well, straining to hear the waves crashing on a shore thousands of miles away; rolling over to put on arm around a body that wasn't there.

He'd always liked sleeping alone before. Liked the rumble of the city.

A knock on the door pulled him back to his surroundings, and he managed to return the snow globe to its place and refocus his attention on the document he was reading before his PA entered the room. His pulse quickened. Had Ellie been in touch? He'd asked Lydia to tell him if she heard from Ellie, but there had been nothing at all in over three weeks.

Was she well? Was she safe? She was probably busy with the shop, with her committees. Busy going to the pub with her friends...with that blond surfer who hadn't been able to keep his eyes off her. As long as it *was* just his eyes.

He made an effort to unclench his jaw. 'Yes?'

'You asked me to let you know when your father was back in his office. He arrived back ten minutes ago.'

'Thanks, Lydia.'

His father had been elusive ever since Max's return to Hartford. Once Max had verified that Great-Aunt Demelza's shares were valid he had done his best to track his father down so he could tell him of the change in ownership in person. It had proved impossible. In the end he had had to notify him by email.

His father hadn't replied.

Max leaned back in his chair and stared at the snow globe. *This was it.* Everything he wanted was within his grasp. He should feel elated, and yet the best word he could find to describe his feelings was hollow.

Empty.

He glanced over at the snow globe again. He swore the penguin was trying to tell him something.

It was a short walk to his father's office, which occupied the other top floor corner suite. Max's great-grandfather had settled in Hartford in the early nineteen-twenties to provide printing services to the city's insurance industry, but had soon branched out into book publishing and journalism. It was Max's grandfather who had taken the company into TV, film, and expanded out of the US.

But although they now had offices around the globe—publishing headquarters in New York, digital in Silicon Valley and Los Angeles—the heart of the operation remained in Connecticut. Where it had all begun.

The door to his father's office was closed but Max didn't knock, simply twisting the handle and walking in. To his surprise his father wasn't at his desk; he was standing at the window, looking out over the river beyond, his shoulders slumped. Would he concede defeat before the battle began?

Max hoped so. It might be necessary, but he had no stomach for this fight.

'Hi, Dad.'

'Max.' The shoulders straightened, and his expression as he turned around was one of familiar paternal affability. 'Good vacation? Where did you go? Cornwall?'

As if he didn't already know.

'I wasn't on holiday. I was in London and sorting out Great-Aunt Demelza's estate. Did you know she lived in the house your grandfather was born in? She left it to me. It's pretty special.'

'Are you going to sell it?'

That was his father. Not a trace of sentimentality.

Max closed his eyes briefly and saw the round white house perched high above the harbour, the golden wood of the polished floorboards, that spectacular view. 'No. I'm thinking of keeping it.'

Ellie's words floated through his head. *'The village needs young families not more second home owners.'* It might be a selfish decision but it was the right one. For now, at least.

'It wasn't all that she left me, Dad.'

His father's jaw tightened. 'Apparently not. The papers…they're legitimate?'

'Seems so. You realise what that means?'

'That we're equal partners. Well, you *are* my

son, although it seems a bit premature for you to have so much control. You're still just a boy.'

Max breathed in, willing himself not to rise to the bait. 'We need to talk, Dad. Want to take a walk?'

Hartford, like many cities, had a gritty side, and many affluent families, like Max's own, preferred to live outside the city in large estates by the river, or in one of the quaint and historic small Connecticut towns.

But since he had moved into one of the many luxury apartment blocks catering for young professionals Max had grown fond of the old city, especially enjoying the riverside paths and parks which were vibrant public spaces, perfect for walking, running and cycling. He steered his father towards the river, glad to be outside—even if the temperature *was* hitting the high eighties.

He was even more glad that, unlike his father, he had taken advantage of the company's Dress-down Friday policy and was comfortable in dark khakis and a short-sleeved white shirt.

The park was full of people: families picnicking, personal trainers putting their clients through their moves, couples lying in the sun. Steven Loveday looked around at the buzzing space in obvious surprise. He probably never walked in the city, Max realised. He would be driven in to the office, to the theatre, to the high-end restaurants he frequented, but otherwise he spent his life on his estate or at his club.

'This is all rather nice.' He followed Max down the steep steps and onto the path. 'I had no idea this was here.'

'I guess you wouldn't have.' Max wanted this talk, had sought it out, but now it was time he was finding it hard to find the right words. 'I spoke to Mom.'

A smile spread across his father's face and he clapped Max on the shoulder. 'That's my boy. Has she seen sense?'

'I spoke to Mom and I told her exactly what I am about to tell you.' Max kept his voice level. 'It's not my place to arbitrate your divorce. That's between you guys. Personally, I think you need to go and talk to her face to face. She deserves that courtesy, at least.'

Steven Loveday stood still, incongruous in his

hand-made suit amongst the rollerbladers, joggers and families. 'Right...' he said slowly.

'She won't come after the company.' Max took a deep breath. *Here goes.* 'As long as I'm in charge.'

His father looked at him blankly. 'What?'

'Dad, our profits are down. We're losing some of our most valuable staff. Rumours are flying through the industry that we're on the brink of collapse. The publishers tell me that agents aren't entertaining our bids. We're losing ground.'

His father waved a hand, dismissing the litany of disasters. 'That was bound to happen after your grandfather died. We knew there would be some instability.'

'It's been over a year.'

'We have a strategy.'

'*No.* No, Dad, there isn't a strategy. I don't know what we're doing, the board doesn't know, and none of our senior directors have any direction. You're on a spending spree and I spend my whole time firefighting. It's not a strategy. It's a disaster.'

'Come on, Max, things are a little tight...'

‘I own fifty per cent outright.’ There was no point rehashing the same old arguments. ‘You own twenty-five per cent, with an interest in the other twenty-five. Your share is yours. You can do what you like with it. But I want you to sign the other share over to me now. Not when you retire. If you do then Mom will leave the company alone. The rest of the settlement is up to you two—but you owe her, and I think you know it.’

His father’s eyes narrowed. ‘And if I won’t?’

‘Then I’ll go to the board and force a vote. I’m pretty confident that they’ll back me.’

His father started walking slowly along the path. The colour had left his face and he looked every minute of his fifty-eight years. Guilt punched through Max but he ignored it. It was time Steven Loveday faced the consequences of his actions.

‘Dad, you are about to have another baby. A chance to do it all over again.’ Max didn’t add *to do it right*, but the unsaid words hung uncomfortably in the air. ‘You say you love Mandy. I hope you do. I hope for all our sakes that this time it’s real. Spend time with her…with the baby.’

'Take early retirement? That would be convenient.' His father's words were laced with scorn.

'Or take an executive role. Dad, honestly, are you enjoying it? Running DL Media? Does it buzz through your brains? Is it the first thing you think of when you wake up, before you sleep?'

'Well...I...'

'Or do you miss the afternoons golfing, the long lunches? It's okay if you do, Dad. I'm just saying that running DL is all-consuming. And I don't think that's what you want.'

'And you do? You want to be like your grandfather? Work first and the rest of the world be damned?'

Max looked away, across the river. 'It's all I know. All I want.'

At least it had been. But it hadn't been work occupying his mind as he lay in bed fruitlessly chasing sleep over the last few weeks.

It had been a small terraced building on a steep road and the dark-eyed, toffee-haired girl who occupied it.

She hadn't been born and brought up in his world. She didn't know the rules.

She had no interest in timetables.

But when he imagined his future she was all that he could see.

'I don't see that I have much choice. You've won, Max. I hope it's all you want it to be.'

His father turned and walked away, leaving Max alone by the river.

He should be elated. The company was his. He had won.

But he had no one to tell, no one to celebrate with. He was all alone, and the only person he wanted to share his news with was on the other side of the Atlantic.

Maybe she should get a dog. Something to walk on the beach with, something to talk to. Uncritical adoration.

Ellie breathed in and turned slowly. The briny air filled her lungs and her eyes drank in the deep blue of a summer ocean. The roaring of the waves filled her ears. Trengarth on an idyllic summer's day.

It was perfect, and yet somehow it didn't fill her with the usual peace. Discomfort was gnawing away at her and she couldn't assuage it. Not with work—the shop seemed to run itself these days. Not with the festival—thanks to the brilliant volunteers making sure not a single task remained to be done. And now not even a walk on the beach helped.

Max was right. Watching wasn't enough. But she had been on the sidelines for so long. How could she step out onto the crest of a wave?

She stepped back onto the road, for once not turning back to admire the view.

'Hi, Ellie, are you walking back? I'm going that way.' Sam was breathing hard as he caught up with her.

'You are?' Ellie looked at Sam in surprise. 'Don't you live in the old town?'

'Yeah, but I have some business on the hill.' He looked vaguely uncomfortable.

She had seen a great deal of Sam recently. He'd been walking on the beach at the same time as she had several evenings recently and always joined her. Twice he had been at The Boat House when she'd popped in for her regular Friday lunch and he'd asked her to sit with him. He was on the organising committee, on her pub quiz team. He had popped in to the shop several times, to buy presents or ask for recommendations.

They'd laughed about how they must stop bumping into each other all the time. And here they were. Again.

Ellie's stomach swooped and it was all she could do to keep walking and talking normally. She'd suspected that he liked her before. But now she was sure. He *liked* her liked her.

Her hands felt too big, her legs too long, her laugh too grating. She was hyper-aware of her every word and gesture. They all seemed clumsy and fake. *Breathe,* she told herself crossly. *Max* liked *you liked you and that didn't worry you.*

And Sam was great. A catch. He had an interesting job, he was funny, community-minded. He was handsome enough, if you liked fit, blue-eyed, blond-haired surfer guys.

Did she?

Or was she a little too fixated on dark-haired, caramel-eyed Americans?

Unobtainable dark-haired Americans.

She was supposed to be moving on.

'Sorry, what was that?' Sam had been speaking and she hadn't even heard him.

'The festival,' he repeated. 'It's going well.'

'It seems to be,' she agreed cautiously. 'Obviously it's early days yet, and we have a long way to go, but DL's London office have been really helpful. I think we're guaranteed some big names through them anyway, so that should put us on the map.'

Her phone beeped at this opportune moment and, thankful for the interruption, she smiled at Sam apologetically. 'I should get this. Go on without me. Honestly.'

He looked as if he might protest, but she turned away, pulling her phone out of her pocket as she did so. At some point she was going to have to let him know she wasn't interested.

Because she *wasn't* interested. Although how she wished she was. Darn Max Loveday. He was supposed to be the cure, not the poison.

The number on her phone was a London one, which wasn't unusual these days. She had never spent so much time on the phone, mainly to agents or publishers, trying to secure the names she wanted whilst considering the ones they were pushing at her. It was a real game of nerves, and to her surprise she got a buzz out of the negotiations.

'Hello?'

'Ellie? It's Andy Taylor here, Head of Retail Marketing at DL Media. We met at the industry awards the other week.'

'Hi, Andy. Is this about the festival? Because all my paperwork is back at the shop.' She dimly remembered him, but he wasn't one of her usual contacts.

'Festival? No, no. Actually, Ellie, I was calling you on the off-chance that you might be interested in a job. We have an opening here at DL Media and I think you might be the perfect candidate.'

Ellie stood in the street, time slowing down, until all she could hear was the slow thumping of her heart. Even the cry of the gulls, the chatter of children outside the ice cream shop faded away. That irritating, interfering man. Did Max have to try and sort out *everything*?

'Did Max put you up to this?'

'Max? You mean Max Loveday?' Andy Taylor laughed. 'Oh, no. He doesn't interfere at all with local staff, or any hiring below director level. No, it's your experience we're interested in.'

'My experience?'

Stop repeating things, Ellie or he'll change his mind.

'It's a retail marketing role. Obviously you run a really successful shop in a remote area, and I think that means you'd be able to bring a really valuable perspective to the role.'

He did? Ellie's heart and lungs seemed to expand, filling her chest with almost unbearable pressure. Her hard work had been noticed, appreciated.

'I know you live in Cornwall, and your shop is there, and this would be a really big change. But although this is a London-based post there would be some flexibility about working at home: maybe one or two days a week, depending on schedules. If that was what you wanted. Would you be free to come in next week and have a chat about it?'

Ellie looked around at the dear, familiar village. The harbour curved in front of her. Just up the road was her own shop, her sanctuary. Her safety net. Could she leave it? Move on?

She swallowed, trying to get moisture back into her dry mouth, her stomach twisting.

But she had felt at home on the South Bank hadn't she? Had wondered what it would be like to be one of that confident sea of people at home in the city. Here was her opportunity to find out—and if it didn't work out she could always come back to the shop.

Besides, she might not even get the job. It was an interview…that was all.

'Next week is fine. The twenty-first? Yes, I'll see you then.'

See: she didn't need Max Loveday to move on. She didn't need him and one day soon she would stop wanting him too.

CHAPTER TWELVE

IT MADE ABSOLUTELY no sense to come all the way to London for just one day. Ellie had travelled up the night before her interview to make sure she was rested, on time and not too travel stained, although it was hard to look at her small, practical, budget hotel room and not yearn, just a little, for the opulence of the hotel suite she had occupied on her last London trip.

And as she had made the journey she might as well stay another day. Do some more sight-seeing while she mulled over her next move. So here she was. With time on her hands. A tourist once again.

A tourist with a purpose. She was going to walk around central London and work out whether she could live here or not, even on a part-time basis.

The interview had gone well. *Really* well. More of an informal chat than a terrifying interrogation. She had found herself enjoying the experience and had to admit that the job, being a liaison between small independent shops and the publishers, sounded fascinating.

From the interviewers' enthusiasm and attention to detail Ellie was pretty sure they were going to offer her the role. She was also pretty sure that she would take it, with the proviso that she worked at least one day a week in Cornwall. Apparently plenty of people let out rooms on a weekday-only basis, and with two five-hour commutes in her week she would have plenty of time to catch up on paperwork.

Of course she would be insanely busy. She would have to appoint a shop manager, but she'd still do the accounts and work weekends, plus there was the festival. But she was young, healthy and oh, so single.

Ellie picked up her bag. That was it. She was on the verge of a new, exciting, dream-fulfilling experience and she would not mope around pathetically, thinking about holding hands on the South Bank. She was going to leave this perfectly adequate hotel room and she was going to have some fun whether she felt like it or not.

It was a warm, humid day, the sun hidden by low white cloud. Ellie hesitated outside the hotel's modest entrance, unsure which way to turn. Parks, palaces, museums, shops, exhibitions, theatres—the whole city was open to her.

It was almost paralysing, all this choice. She hadn't felt this way before, when she'd been here with Max. Then having no plan, no destination, had been exciting...an adventure. How was she going to travel and see all the places she had always dreamed of if she couldn't even walk down the street in her own capital city without panicking?

Ellie lifted her chin. Of course she could do it.

She set off almost blindly, walking through the bustling city streets. Four weeks since he had left. More than twice as long as she had actually known him. It made absolutely no sense that she missed him so badly. That it felt as if something fundamental was missing...some part of her like her liver or her lungs. Or her heart.

It made no sense that she instinctively looked

for his ironic smile when committee meetings were particularly dull, that she missed his hand in hers on the beach. That she reached for him in her sleep.

He was the first person she wanted to tell when her mother called with updates on Bill's health. The person she wanted to share the amazing book she had just read with. The person she wanted to be sitting opposite her, coffee in hand, book open, reading in companionable silence.

It made no sense at all. But there it was.

Ellie had reached her destination. One huge shop, five storeys high, filled with books, books, nothing but books. It was a mecca for the bookworm, a source of inspiration for a fellow bookshop owner. She should be filled with anticipation, with the tingle in her fingers and the tightening of excitement in her stomach that exploring a new bookshop gave her.

Nothing. Not even a twinge.

Two hours later she emerged.

Five floors and she hadn't felt breathless once. Not a single display had moved her. She hadn't bought one book. Even the expensive piece of cake in the café had tasted of nothing.

It was no good. She was on the verge of an exciting new life and it was if she were dead inside. She needed to recapture some of that heady excitement from her last trip here. Maybe she should head back to the South Bank and see how much she enjoyed hanging out there in the daytime and on her own. See whether she really wanted to live half her life in the anonymity of the city.

Ellie couldn't walk at her usual rate. It was too hot and the tourists were out in force, stopping in front of her, ambling along and taking selfies at every landmark, no matter how insignificant. But it didn't take her long to reach Westminster Bridge. Last time she had walked over the bridge she had been holding Max's hand, with the promise of his kiss hanging over her like a velvet cloak; rich, decadent and all-encompassing.

In front of her the London Eye dominated the skyline. Ellie stopped in the middle of the bridge, her hands on the railings as she looked down at the wide swell of the Thames. So she missed him? That much was clear. The real question was, what was she going to do about it?

Slowly she retraced their steps, across the bridge and down the steps. The queue for the London Eye was already long and she scanned it eagerly. Hoping to see what? Their shadows? A faint wisp of Ellie and Max, still laughing in the queue?

No. No more mooning around looking for the ghosts of lovers past. She pulled her gaze away and marched on, only to be confronted by another queue. The queue for the London Aquarium. The missing piece from their last trip.

If she went in she would go alone. That had never been the deal. She should just walk on by, carry on with her plans. But her feet were heavy, her legs reluctant to move. Ellie stood still, tourists weaving around her, racked with indecision. Maybe she *should* go in. Her last and final act of being pathetic before she pulled herself together and thought about whether she wanted this job or not and where she wanted her life to go.

Just a few small decisions to make.

And then she saw it. A poster advertising tea

with the penguins. *Today.* 'Diary it in,' he had said. Of course it had been a joke...a meaningless comment.

But still. It was a sign. She wasn't sure exactly what the sign meant, but no matter. A sign was a sign.

The queue to get in was ridiculous.

If Max had been there, there was no way he'd have queued. He'd have paid top-dollar for a priority pass and probably been conveyed in on a chariot pulled by walruses. It must be nice to be rich.

Still, she was near the front at last. It was only a quarter to twelve, and she might as well enjoy the whole experience as she was there. Obviously there were several aquariums, zoos and animal sanctuaries a lot closer to home, but that wasn't the point. At all.

No, the point was that she was proving a point. She was taking a positive step. Taking control of her own destiny one very slow step at a time.

Finally she was at the front of the queue. Ellie's heart began to hammer.

'Oh, I'm sorry.' The girl behind the desk didn't look that sorry. She looked busy and tired and fraught. 'The tea with the penguins is all booked out. Do you want a normal ticket?'

Ellie stared. She had blown it. She couldn't even make a melodramatic gesture without messing it up.

'Miss?'

Ellie sighed and held out her bank card. She was here after all. 'Just one adult ticket, please.'

It didn't get easier once she was inside. The entrance was crowded with buggies, harassed families and small children slipping out of their parents' grasps to run amok. And everyone moved so *slowly*! You'd think they'd paid a fortune to look at each and every exhibit, to read all the noticeboards and interpretations, to watch the sharks feeding.

Actually, *that* was quite cool. But, no, she wasn't here to look at sharks.

Finally, *finally,* she managed to sidle past a large group, dodge a particularly active toddler and navigate her way through a group of texting teens. And there she was. At the entrance to the penguin room.

It was like entering an ice palace. White walls, white ceilings and low blue lighting. Windows on one side separated the black and white flightless birds from the spellbound watchers, giving them space to swim and play in peace. She felt a moment's pang for them, confined to this artificial room, unable to explore the wider seas, but at least they were safe from orcas and other predators.

For one long moment Ellie forgot why she was there, swept up in the icy atmosphere and the sheer wonder of the penguins, so graceful in the water, so comical on land. But she soon remembered her purpose and looked around. The room was busy, apart from a cordoned-off area by one of the viewing windows where several tables and chairs were set up. Cake stands and tea sets were neatly arranged on the tables.

Ellie inhaled, long and deep. There was no way he would have remembered that throw-away comment—and even if he had there was no reason for him to be here. But a quick look wouldn't hurt. Would it?

Of course he wasn't there.

Her chest tightened. Should she be disappointed? Heartbroken? Relieved?

Ellie watched a penguin dive into the water, its body hurtling at speed towards the pool floor before executing a neat turn and zooming back up to the surface. The truth was that she was none of the above.

She was determined.

She had queued for nearly an hour on a hot, humid day, and fought her way through the crowds. Not because she had expected to see Max; it wasn't even that she'd *hoped* to see him, amazing as it would have been if he was actually here. No, she had come here to work out what she wanted. It wasn't the most heroic quest of all times, sure. She hadn't fought a Minotaur or anything. But she had tested herself, tested her commitment, and now she knew.

Knew that there was no point leaving her happiness in the hands of fate, or hoping that coincidence would send Max back her way. If she wanted a life with Max Loveday she was going to have to go after it. Show him that she was no damsel in distress but an equal—and a far better match than some well-bred society girl who might know all the right people but would bore him to death within six months.

Really, she was going to be the one who saved him.

So that meant she needed to book her first flight abroad on her own. It wasn't going to be Paris or Rome. She was heading to the States.

Max leaned back in his chair and watched Ellie. His first incredulous happiness at seeing that she was actually here hadn't faded, but it was joined by amusement now as he watched her. Her jaw was set and she looked grimly determined.

He hoped that boded well for him. She might be planning his disembowelment.

'Excuse me.' He walked over to her, stopping behind her as if he were just another visitor, trying to find a spot to view the penguins. 'Are you meeting someone for afternoon tea? I have a table for two, right over here.'

'Max!' She whirled round, her hands against his chest, whether to ward him off or check he was real he didn't know. 'What are you doing here?'

'Afternoon tea, remember? Only they don't serve sushi. Apparently it would be a little insensitive in an aquarium. You can see their point…'

'Yes.' She bit her lip, her face an adorable mixture of confusion and joy. 'But it wasn't a real date. It was a joke.'

'Yet here you are.'

'I was in London anyway, so I thought…you know…while I was here I might as well come and…'

'See if I was here?'

'No.' Her cheeks were turning an interesting shade of red. 'I wanted to see the penguins.'

'And?'

'And what?'

He lowered his voice. 'Are they everything you hoped they would be?'

Her eyes were serious as they scanned his face. 'I'm not sure yet. I hope so. What about you? Are they living up to expectations?'

Max stared down at her, at the pointed chin, the delicate cheekbones, the candid brown eyes. 'Oh, yes...' Was that him? So hoarse? 'Everything I dreamed of.'

Her eyes fell, but not before he saw the spark of hope in them. 'You're sure?'

He took one of her hands in his. 'I've never been surer.'

At one level Max was aware that they were blocking a window, that people were moving past them, trying to look over their heads. That other conversations were taking place, children were crying, asking questions, pushing past him. But it was as if there was a bubble enclosing Ellie and him. They were in the room and yet apart from it. In an alternative universe of two.

He watched her inhale before she looked back up at him.

'What about your parents and DL?'

'Don't let it overwhelm you, but you are looking at the new CEO of DL Media. My father has decided to take an executive board position.'

She raised her elegantly arched brows. 'Decided?'

'That's the official line. As for the divorce: I'm out of it. My only request is that they behave themselves when they have to be in the same room.' He paused. 'At my wedding, for instance.'

Her lips parted. 'Your wedding?'

He held her hand just a little bit tighter. 'There's nothing worse than feuding exes at a wedding. Apart from midlife-crisis-suffering uncles hitting on the bridesmaids, that is. Don't you think?'

'I haven't really thought about it. Are you planning ahead, or have you brought your timetable forward?'

'I got rid of the whole damn timetable. Turns out you can plan for everything but love, Ellie.'

'Love?'

Was that a crack in her voice? He couldn't wait any longer. He'd spent the last eight hours practising elegant speeches but they had gone straight out of his head.

'I can be based in the London office most of the time. Obviously I'd need to go to Hartford regularly, travel a lot, but the UK would be my main home. I'd buy a place in London but spend weekends at The Round House, work from there whenever I could. Get that boat, walk on the beach, win the pub quiz. If you want to, that is?'

'Do I want to win the pub quiz?' Her voice was teasing but her eyes told a different story, shining with happiness. 'I already did. Twice.'

'But not on *my* team. And that's where I want you, Ellie. On my team—and I'll be on yours. For ever. I know it's fast, and I know I didn't make the best first impression, and I know you want time to work out who you are, and I respect that—'

He came to a halt as she put a cool finger to his lips. 'Max Loveday, stop babbling and tell me what you want.'

'I want to marry you, Ellie. Preferably right away. But I'll wait. We can take it as slow as you like.'

'That's a shame.' She stepped a little closer, one hand still in his, her other hand moving from his mouth to cup his cheek. 'Because I don't want to take it slow at all. I want to do it all, Max. Marriage, travel, babies, work. I want it all.'

'You do?'

She nodded solemnly. 'Although you might

have to put up with me at more than just the weekends. I might be working in London during the week as well. Does that ruin your carefully thought out plans?'

'I'm learning to be adaptable. London? Really?' His mouth curved into a tender smile. 'Just when I thought you couldn't surprise me more.'

She narrowed her eyes. 'I was interviewed for a job at DL Media today. That didn't have anything to do with *you*, did it?'

'Not a thing. But I'll write you a reference. Although I'm not sure fiancés are acceptable referees, even if they *do* own the company.'

'Fiancé?'

She folded her arms. His cheek still tingled where she had touched it.

'I don't remember you asking. Not properly.'

He reached into his pocket. 'I don't have a ring,' he warned her. 'I want it to be perfect and exactly what you want.' He pulled out a box and dropped down on to one knee.

'Max! Get up!'

'What's that man doing, Mummy?'

Max was horrifyingly aware that the penguins

were no longer the main attraction. The room was full of people and they were all looking, smiling and staring at him. Oh, no—phones were out and pointed in their direction. She'd better say yes.

He took her hand, and as soon as he touched her he was back in the bubble. Let them watch and film.

'Ellie Scott, I love you and I want to give you the world. Will you marry me?'

He held up the box.

'I thought you said you didn't have a ring?' Her voice trembled as she took it from him.

'Open it.'

She slowly lifted the lid. 'It's a snow globe.'

'I had it made specially. Look inside, Ellie, what can you see?'

'Oh, the Eiffel Tower! And is that the Coliseum? And the Sydney Opera House? Does it snow in Sydney?'

'I'll take you to all those places and a hundred besides. We'll walk through the streets and eat in little neighbourhood restaurants and get to the heart of everywhere we go. If we go together. Will you, Ellie?'

'Yes, Max. Of course I will. I'll go anywhere as long as you are with me.'

He got up and cupped her face in his hands. 'Are you sure, Ellie?'

'I'm completely sure. I love you, Max Loveday. All my life I've been too scared to reach out for what I want, but not any more. You've shown me that I can do anything I want to. And what I really want is to spend the rest of my life with you.'

* * * * *

MILLS & BOON®

Large Print – December 2015

The Greek Demands His Heir
Lynne Graham

The Sinner's Marriage Redemption
Annie West

His Sicilian Cinderella
Carol Marinelli

Captivated by the Greek
Julia James

The Perfect Cazorla Wife
Michelle Smart

Claimed for His Duty
Tara Pammi

The Marakaios Baby
Kate Hewitt

Return of the Italian Tycoon
Jennifer Faye

His Unforgettable Fiancée
Teresa Carpenter

Hired by the Brooding Billionaire
Kandy Shepherd

A Will, a Wish...a Proposal
Jessica Gilmore

1115 Rom LP